30-DAY PASS

PETE
FANNING

IMMORTAL WORKS
SALT LAKE CITY

Immortal Works LLC
1505 Glenrose Drive
Salt Lake City, Utah 84104
Tel: (385) 202-0116

Cover Art by Ashley Literski
http://strangedevotion.wixsite.com/strangedesigns

ISBN 978-1-953491-84-8 (Paperback)
ASIN B0D7YW9MDB (Kindle)

To Simon

CHAPTER ONE

Levi wasn't exactly wandering. His mother had specifically warned him against it when they'd pulled into the parking lot of the Med First Center on busy Crawford Road. She'd repeated the warning when they were in the waiting room, as she'd been filling out an insurance form and Levi had asked if he could wait in the car rather than flipping through the mind-numbing magazines on the end tables.

Now, as cars whizzed down the street in both directions and Levi was nearly creamed by a Honda making a screeching left turn, he reminded himself that he wasn't wandering. He knew where he was going. He had a destination.

The Honda driver laid on the horn. Levi sprinted to the other side of the street and didn't slow down until he was crossing the lines marking empty parking spaces in the split and cracked lot of mostly abandoned buildings.

While Levi was worried about his mom—she'd been complaining about her wrist for a few days—he hoped it was only a sprain and they would give her one of those splints and she'd be good to go. But for now, he needed to get a better look at the karate place that had caught his attention the last time they were at Med First.

Whatever Kmart used to be, it was deserted now. Only a few straggling shopping carts remained on the sidewalk amidst some overgrown weeds turned bushes. All the action was at the smaller building to the left, where a cluster of cars sat in the lot.

Levi cut that way, where he came up the sidewalk, stopping just short of the floor to ceiling windows. He could hear shouts of *Hi-ya* from inside as he approached.

His heart was still pounding from the close call with the car at the intersection. But as he edged up close to the window, he managed to hold his breath so he could hear. A deep, confident voice had control of the room.

"Respect. We will always respect one another when we are on the mat. Or off the mat. You represent Kick City out there, and I expect you to always carry yourself with dignity and respect. Yes, sir?"

A resounding "Yes, sir!" caused Levi to start. He leaned just a bit closer to get a better view.

"Okay, let's warm up. Run in place."

It was like a stampede. Levi could feel the movement through the wall. He couldn't take it anymore. Craning his neck, he used his hands to cover the glare as he watched through the window. There weren't as many as he was expecting from the noise, but the eight or so students were all dressed in white robes with colorful belts, jogging in place with their fists up and ready. The instructor was front and center, clad in all black. He, too, was jogging.

"Hit the floor!"

Down they went, then popped back up. As they ran in place, one of the students turned toward the glass and spotted Levi, who pulled away and sucked in a breath.

"Eric, something got your attention?"

"No, sir."

Levi stayed put, out of view from the class. Another thump to the floor, the precise movement of the students working in unison. He kept his back against the wall until the running stopped.

When he managed to peek again, they were throwing kicks. Some were great, others not so much. But a few students were kicking over the heads of their partners. It reminded Levi of some kung fu movies he'd watched at his cousin Jace's house.

His heart sped up. He bounced on his heels. Caught up in the moment, Levi let out a "Hi-ya!" and swung his leg around. *Yeah,* he thought, *I got this.*

He did his best to mimic the students. He set his feet according to the stances he had seen on the floor. Levi became so involved throwing those kicks, and a few punches, that he lost track of time. He switched legs, swung around, then back again. It felt good to move, to kick and punch. He did his best to fend off the imaginary attacker in front of him. Levi didn't hear the door open or notice the instructor watching him until he turned and nearly jumped out of his clothes.

"Not bad. Not bad at all," the instructor said with a smile.

Levi's first impulse was to run. Just bolt between the cars in the parking lot and hope to make it across the street in one piece. But something about the instructor put him at ease. Lean and fit, shifty and sharp, even his hair was pointy, like it refused to sit. Besides, this seemed like the kind of guy who would have no trouble chasing him down. Even if he was barefoot. Levi knew he was busted.

"Oh, I was just..." Levi glanced down at the sidewalk.

The instructor nodded his head toward the classroom. "You want to come in and watch?" He wiggled his eyebrows. "Or participate?"

Participate? Was this guy serious? Levi glanced up to

Crawford Road. "I can't. My mom is..." He nodded toward the busy street.

The instructor looked over his shoulder. "Your mom isn't here?"

"No, she is. She's at the Med First place. I was just wandering around." Did he really just say that?

The instructor frowned. "Okay, but you gotta be careful. That's a busy street. How old are you?"

"Twelve."

The man glanced back inside. Another instructor, this one wearing a blue top unlike all the other white tops in the class, took over the lesson.

"Does your mom have a phone on her? You could call."

Levi shook his head. He didn't want to worry his mom any more than he had to. "No, that's okay. Thanks anyway. I gotta run."

"Okay, but hey, anytime you want to come, the door is open. I can give you thirty days free. Sound like fun?"

Thirty days of karate? Levi couldn't help his smile. "Yeah, that sounds awesome."

"Great." The instructor handed him a card. "Here's your free pass. Come back with your mom. I think you already got the kick going," he said with a laugh. He peeked inside, then came all the way out of the building, letting the door shut behind him. He motioned toward Levi. "You know what? Let me see that again."

Levi flushed with embarrassment. A few of the karate students were watching now, and it dawned on him that he had no idea what he was doing. Still, something about the instructor, the kicks—it felt right, like it was something he knew without knowing. "Uh, okay."

Without thinking on it much more, he let fly and threw his best kick, trying to imitate what he'd watched.

"Wow. Nice! Very nice. Here, do me a favor and pivot your back foot. Like this. Here."

Before he knew it, Levi was taking his first lesson out on the sidewalk. The instructor, whose card said "Mr. Anderson," showed him something called right side guard. He taught him where to place his feet and set his hands. Then he explained again how to pivot, bring his knee up, fold, and set the kick up so it packed the most power. Levi hoped he did okay, even if he did stumble back a few times.

When they were done, Mr. Anderson stood straight and offered a high five. "That's your first lesson right there. And an advanced one at that. We usually don't get to kicking until yellow belt, so nice job."

"Thanks."

Mr. Anderson's smile broadened. His eyes were bright and seemed charged with energy. "Let me see it one more time. Right side guard."

Levi shuffled into position.

The door opened and the other instructor appeared. "Mr. Anderson, we need you for something." The instructor glanced at Levi and smiled. "Well, when you're free."

"Hey, Mr. Tabb, watch this." Mr. Anderson nodded at Levi. "Levi, show him that flip kick."

"Flip kick?" Mr. Tabb raised his eyebrows. "Levi?"

Mr. Anderson smiled. "Oh, yeah." He motioned to Levi and shouted, "Go!"

Levi launched into action. He did exactly what he'd been instructed to do. He threw the kick as high as he could without falling over.

Mr. Tabb set his head back, his brow up. "Very nice." Then, to Mr. Anderson. "This just some kid off the street?"

"Literally. Well, on the sidewalk." He winked at Levi. "Caught him peeking in the windows."

Levi's cheeks blazed warm.

Mr. Anderson smiled, but Mr. Tabb didn't seem so convinced. "You've never taken karate?"

"Just what my cousin showed me."

"And your cousin took karate?"

"Not exactly, but he watched a lot of karate movies."

The two men found this hilarious. Another high five from Mr. Anderson, who then bowed. "Okay, I have to get back to my class. Please," he said, nodding to the pass.

Levi read the words, *Respect. Training. Self-Defense.*

"Take advantage of that. Next class is at six pm on Wednesday. And be careful crossing that street."

"I will. I mean, yes, sir."

Once the instructors got back to class, Levi looked over the pass once more and then started back. He stared at the card the whole way out of the lot, until he figured he really would be careful, mostly not to lose the card as he sprinted across the street at a red light.

He got back to the Med First Center and found his mother outside, wearing a splint on her left hand and looking worried. "Levi, where in the world have you been?"

"Hey, Mom," he said, his thumb pressing on the corner of the card in the pocket of his hoodie, his breaths colliding, getting jumbled up as studied the brace on his mother's wrist. "How is it?" He nodded to her arm.

"Sprained. I'll be okay. Did you cross the street?"

"Mom, I have to show you something."

And right there, as the cars raced past them and the sun went low and golden, Levi performed his kicks the best he could.

His mom's eyes widened some. She told him they were excellent. Then, glancing across the street, her face resettled into its usual position somewhere between worry and exhaustion. "Karate? When did you get interested in karate?"

"Just now," he said, a slight lie.

"Well, kid, I hate to break it to you," she said, starting for the car, "but karate is awfully expensive. We can't afford it."

"Yeah." Levi expected this. "Well, the instructor gave me a thirty-day pass." He presented the card.

His mother took the card and looked it over. "Self-defense, huh?" She handed it back and went looking for her keys with her good hand. "You having some trouble at school, Levi? You feel like you need to protect yourself?"

No, he thought, glancing at her wrist. *But I need to protect you.*

CHAPTER TWO

Mr. Anderson looked over the flushed faces of the students standing before him. Their chests heaved from the pushups and sit-ups, a few burpees thrown in for good measure.

"At ease."

With a collective sigh, the students set their hands behind their backs as they awaited instruction. Mr. Anderson stepped toward the window, where a few minutes ago some kid off the street had executed a nearly flawless flip kick like he'd been doing it all his life.

The dojo was Mr. Anderson's dream. A vision that began the first time he set foot on the mat. And now here he was, at the ripe old age of thirty, with his own studio.

Only at times, more recently, things were more business than karate.

A world champion competitor, Mr. Anderson had gotten where he was through sheer grit and determination. Well, if he was being honest, he'd had some help along the way. Help that had come after his father passed, after his fourth fist fight at school. Help that had saved his life.

Mr. Anderson dove into this oft told story with the class. How he'd been fifteen years old and suspended from high school for the second time in a year, destined for jail, if not something worse, when Master Keaton, an eighth degree black belt, had taken him under his wing and allowed him to basically live at the karate dojo where he honed his craft.

"Master Keaton gave me the instruction," he told the class, tapping at his chest. "But I had to do the work. You have to want it."

Mr. Anderson told this story whenever he had the chance. Not to brag of his accomplishments, but to inspire, to give his students hope and let them know what could be done if they stuck with it. Master Keaton had been an incredible instructor. And what Mr. Anderson didn't mention was that Master Keaton had done it for him almost entirely for free. All because he saw something.

"Give back," he'd said.

Saying the words, telling the story, Mr. Anderson couldn't stop thinking about that boy on the sidewalk. Those kicks. Nearly perfect. Imagine what he could do with a little guidance and instruction.

He shook it off. No time for those thoughts now. Here were his students, ready and willing. They deserved his best, and he would give that to them.

"Okay, let's break some boards!"

Mr. Anderson finished class and chatted with parents about an upcoming seminar. He stressed how important it was for the students to practice at home and attend the workshops, as well as the quarterly tournaments. Last year, his top two students had won medals in the regional semis.

But that kid outside. *He could do some damage in sparring.* Mr. Anderson smiled and nodded through a conversation about an upcoming belt graduation. *Levi. That was his name, right?*

He had that fire in his eyes. Some scrapes and bruises that came from being outside and not indoors playing video games. Mr. Anderson knew it when he saw it. He'd seen it in the mirror many years ago.

As the last class came to an end, the parents corralled the kids out in the lot, chatting amongst one another as the doors shut and the engines started, the brake lights of SUVs and vans heading out, Mr. Anderson looked around at the mats. Some were fraying at the edges, needing tape. But that kid, those kicks...

Mr. Tabb caught him staring. "What's on your mind?"

Mr. Anderson smiled. "That kid earlier."

"Lots of kids. You mean David?" Mr. Tabb shrugged. "He'll be ready for graduation. His mom is just a bit...pushy?"

Mr. Anderson chuckled. "No, Demarcus. I mean that kid outside. He had something."

Mr. Tabb picked up a breaking board—actually plastic with a light foamy cover. He slid the pieces together. "Something?"

"Yeah, you saw him, didn't you? Those kicks. We've got kids coming up for black belts that can't kick like that. Heck, we've got actual black belts who can't kick like that."

Demarcus set the board aside. He turned to Mr. Anderson with a slight squint in his eyes, as though trying to figure him out. "Yeah, they were pretty good kicks."

"Pretty good?" Mr. Anderson shook his head. "That was from watching through the window."

"Don't forget the kung fu movies," Mr. Tabb quipped, and they both laughed. He glanced at the sign-in sheet. "I think I know where this is going."

"You do, huh?" Mr. Anderson said. The two men had been working together for nearly five years. Came up the ranks together. Mr. Anderson knew when his friend was messing with him, just like his friend always read what he was thinking.

Sure enough, Mr. Tabb picked up the sheet. "But we're behind in enrollments. I mean, *paid* enrollments. We're last in the state, fifth out of five schools."

"Yeah, what's new there? The other schools are in bigger cities, more kids to choose from."

"So, you want to give the kid a shot?"

"I do."

"Okay, and I hate to say this because of the way it sounds, but did you see how he was dressed? The beat-up tennis shoes. The dirty jeans?"

Mr. Anderson kicked the weight bag. "So, we only recruit rich kids?"

"Not saying that."

"What is this, a country club?"

Mr. Tabb sighed. "Here we go."

Mr. Anderson attacked the bag with a flurry of quick punches before finishing it off with a crisp roundhouse kick. "I started teaching to help, not to become a millionaire."

"Mission accomplished. But we have bills to pay, sir."

Four precise kicks. *Whap, whap, whap, whap.* "I know, I know. Let's just see what happens."

"I think I know already."

Whap!

CHAPTER THREE

L evi threw the kick once more. "Like that, see?"

Gina shook the bangs from her face, glancing up from her phone. "Yeah."

"Did you see?" Levi's shoulders slumped. "You weren't watching."

Gina typed furiously before she looked up again. "Yes. I saw it the first three times you did it."

Levi smiled. "Why don't you try it?"

"Because I don't want to?"

"You should try it. It's fun."

Gina's bracelets jingled as she pocketed the phone. "I'm good, thanks."

The bus rumbled up the hill. Levi hefted his book bag. "Mr. Anderson, the instructor guy, he seemed impressed with my kicking. I'm going back tomorrow. I hope. Mom said she'd take me."

Gina nodded along, struggling with the weight of her bag over her shoulder. Gina's older sister, Heather, wanted to be a hair stylist and experimented on her little sister. This month it was chin length with blue streaks in the bangs, a few spikes in the back. She sort of looked like an anime character, but it was working for her, especially when she scowled, as she did now. "My cousin took karate a few years back. I think he made it to orange belt."

"Why did he quit?" Levi said, stepping onto the bus.

Gina shrugged. "Just got bored. And from what my uncle was saying, it's not cheap, you know?"

They found their usual seats, six rows down. Levi on the left side of the aisle, Gina on the right. The bus hitched and pulled forward, and Levi wondered, not for the first time, what it would be like to have cousins and siblings. Sure, it seemed like they fought all the time, but how nice would it be to come home to a house full of people, noise? Anything but the empty silence Levi found when his mom was pulling swing shifts.

It was a good day, as Noah and Jeremiah sat in the back, focused on who sent what text message instead of their usual pastime of terrorizing kids on the bus. Levi gazed out the window, thinking about cousins and sisters and dads who weren't wild-eyed and didn't like to use family members as a punching bag.

Again, his thoughts meandered back to karate class. He was going to need new socks, as his were gray and had holes in the heels. Maybe he could just walk inside barefoot, or would that be weird? Would he get a robe thing, or was that for students who paid? Probably paid, he figured.

Levi considered little else than karate throughout the day. But he was careful not to mention it to anyone. Only Gina, because she could be trusted to keep a secret. Some people said it was weird that his best friend was a girl, but Levi didn't exactly consider Gina a girl. She was Gina, and they'd been through a ton together.

Occasionally throughout the day, his legs would flex, like they were going to start kicking in class, under his desk. He had to force himself not to throw the new punches he'd learned. All he wanted to do was get back to Kick City and perfect those kicks and punches.

It wasn't until he got home that he started to worry.

Worry number one was that his mother wasn't home yet. Which might be okay, as it was only four and class wasn't until five-thirty. They'd need to leave around five to be safe, with heavy traffic and all. Worry number two was that he had no idea what to wear. He looked in the dirty laundry basket and sniffed out a pair of basketball shorts that were in okay shape.

He scarfed down a bowl of store-brand Cheerios. He did some pushups to warm up, then almost did his math homework, but his brain was buzzing too hard for him to get his bookbag open. He did some kicks instead. Five o'clock came around, and he called his mother's phone but got no answer. More kicks outside. And just as he was set to hike to Kick City, his mother's dented Toyota pulled into the lot.

She had her purse in her lap, reaching for the takeout boxes, when she saw him. "Hey, what's going on with you?"

Levi threw his hands out. "Karate, remember?"

She looked him over. "Oh, we're going?"

"Yes, we're going!" he shouted, then corrected himself. "I mean, please."

His mother sighed. Levi winced at the pang of guilt that came with seeing the brace on her wrist, the lines around her eyes and mouth. How tired she looked. The way the car ticked and hissed and sounded like it wanted to sit right there in the parking lot for the night.

"I really want to try it, Mom. It's free, remember?"

"For now, it's free," she said, her eyes narrowing. "It's how they get you in."

"Mom, don't start."

"Okay, fine. Come on." She set the takeout boxes from work

—spaghetti, Levi guessed, judging by the smell—in the backseat while she warned Levi not to get his hopes up about free lessons.

Sure, his mom said, she was happy he'd found something that interested him. But there was simply no extra money for karate. No extra money period.

Levi promised he would not get his hopes up. And he was telling the truth. As they drove off, Levi wasn't sure his hopes could possibly get any higher anyway.

They pulled into the lot with two minutes to spare. Levi's mom checked her phone. Levi, who'd decided to forgo socks and stuff his bare feet in his worn shoes, took a shaky breath. This was it.

"Do I need to come in?" she asked.

Levi threw his shoulders up and down. "I don't know. I guess. I gotta get in there."

His mother smiled as she wiped at his shirt. "Wow, look at you."

A van pulled up beside them. Three kids, all with orange belts, hopped out hefting huge duffle bags with Kick City patches. They seemed to know exactly what to do and where to go. Levi's mother was still wiping at him, making a fuss over him.

Levi whispered through gritted teeth. "Mom, stop it. Please!"

He climbed out of the car and tried to blend in behind the orange belts. When they stopped at the door and bowed, Levi nearly ran into them.

"Good evening, sir!" they said one by one.

Levi half bowed as he entered but wasn't sure what to do next. Maybe ten kids, all in karate robes with colorful stars on the collar, lined up along the wall from shortest to tallest. The kids at the shortest end looked like kindergartners. They were pushing and shoving playfully. Parents chatted amongst themselves, laughing and nodding casually. Levi stood at the door.

Mr. Anderson was nowhere in sight. Levi ignored the patch of sweat on his back as he glanced out to the lot where his mother was still in the car, on the phone with a bill collector, he guessed, seeing how she was talking with her hands. Levi still had no idea where to go or what to do next. He was about to say forget it and turn for the door when he heard his name.

"Levi? That's it, right?"

He spun around and found Mr. Tabb. Levi smiled, flushed with relief at the sight of a familiar face. "Yeah."

Mr. Tabb cocked his head and raised an eyebrow. "You mean, 'yes, sir'?"

"Yes, um, yes, sir," Levi repeated.

"Good, good. Here at Kick City, we're big on respect. As you walk through that door, you bow. We address the teachers, adults, and parents by sir or ma'am. We say yes sir, no sir, and all that good stuff, got it?"

"Yeah—yes, sir?"

Mr. Tabb did the eyebrow raise again before he smiled and cuffed him on the back. "You'll get there," he said, and Levi exhaled before Mr. Tabb asked, "Is your mom or dad around?"

Levi glanced back to the lot. His mom was really letting someone have it on the phone. No way was he bringing her into the studio when she was all worked up. "Yeah, but she's a little busy."

"Okay, okay. No problem." Mr. Tabb guided Levi toward the other students. "Now, let's get you lined up here. Hmm," he said, sizing Levi up. "Let's put you in right...here. Kevin, Emma, make some room for Levi."

The two kids scooted apart, and Levi fell in place between them. Emma's robe was crisp and clean with a dazzling array of patches and gold stars. Kevin had patches too, not as many but enough to make his robe look cool. Kevin was joking with another kid about Minecraft when Mr. Tabb took control of the class.

"Okay, students. Take the mat."

Levi did his best to follow the others to the numbered tape spots on the mat. He was still wondering where Mr. Anderson was when the back door swung open and the instructor appeared with a smile. His voice took the room by storm.

"Is everyone ready to work?"

A resounding *yes, sir*, filled the room and Levi felt it in his chest. Mr. Anderson bowed before he stepped onto the mat and stood before them. He smiled broadly as he looked them over. Levi did his best to mimic the way the other kids stood, with their hands behind their backs.

Mr. Anderson cracked a few jokes with the parents. He ribbed a kid about his belt hanging too low. When he stopped in front of Levi long enough to nod, Levi swelled with pride. Then he was gone, and it was time to work.

"Hit the floor!"

Of all the fantasies Levi had had in the past twenty-four hours, none of them included being so...winded. He was out of shape, he realized, as he struggled to get through the rounds of pushups and sit-ups and weird stretching positions. His arms burned from the start, and he was thinking he might've made a huge mistake as the class suffered through a round of burpees. It wasn't until they dropped down for splits that Levi found he was able to get to the floor without any problems whatsoever.

"Whoa, Levi," Mr. Tabb called out. "Mr. Anderson, look what we've got over here."

Every face in the room turned to Levi. His cheeks burned as he worried about his filthy feet and kind of dirty shorts. But Mr. Anderson hurried over and kneeled in front of him.

"No wonder you can kick so high. Here, this way." Mr. Anderson helped Levi roll his hips out and sit straight up.

Levi was surprised at the pull in his legs, but he was okay with it.

"All right, people," the instructor said to the class. "You're getting shown up by the new guy." He lectured the class about stretching and how it was crucial to kicking.

Levi breathed a sigh of relief as all the faces turned from him, and he wondered if they'd ever get to a lesson.

Finally, Mr. Anderson had them pair up, and Levi found himself staring at Emma, the girl in the super clean robe, which, he'd learned over the course of class, was called a gi.

Levi heard the words "defense techniques," and to his horror, he realized he was going to have to wrap his arms around Emma so she could break free.

Emma was small and, well, a girl, so Levi wasn't sure how to go about things until Mr. Tabb demonstrated the hold. When it was Levi's turn, he stood behind Emma and gave her the world's faintest hug.

"Hi ya!" In a blink, Emma had wiggled free. Another "hi ya," and she grabbed ahold of Levi's right arm, swung her hip, and flung him onto the mat.

He lay stunned as Emma set a foot on his chest and stood over him, a smirky smile on her face, before she offered a hand to help him up.

Mr. Anderson clapped his hands. "Don't look so surprised, Levi. This is karate."

Levi closed his eyes.

Mr. Anderson took him by the shoulders. "Rule number one: don't underestimate your opponent. And besides," he said, shoving Emma playfully. "Emma's tough, probably the toughest student in here. Don't be fooled by that bow in her hair."

Levi didn't argue, and again, Mr. Tabb worked with him to

show him the maneuver. Soon, he and Emma were taking turns slinging each other to the mat. Levi was sweating by the time the lesson ended and they returned to their spots on the floor.

Once the drills started, class flew by, and Levi was surprised to see his mother by the door, looking on with a bemused expression, even whipping out her phone to take a picture when Mr. Anderson called Levi up to present him with a white belt.

Cheeks aflame, Levi accepted the belt with a bow before Mr. Anderson tied it up and they bowed again. To Levi's surprise, none of the kids snickered or laughed like they would have at school. In fact, they cheered, which surprised him as much as being thrown to the mat by a girl.

They were bowing off the mat when Mr. Anderson called Levi back. "You have a minute?"

Levi knew his mom would be in a rush to get home, but she relented, and they followed Mr. Anderson through a door to the back of the studio, to a regular office with a computer and pictures and a calendar and piles of notes everywhere. Levi didn't know what he'd been expecting, swords and nun chucks maybe, but not office stuff.

Mr. Anderson offered them a seat and sat across from them. "How did you enjoy class?"

Levi nodded. "I liked it. Sir."

The instructor chuckled. "You did well. Again, Emma is one of our top students. And don't think just because she's a girl she won't rough you up. Some of our best sparrers are girls."

Mr. Anderson introduced himself to Levi's mom. She clutched her purse with her good hand, her eyes narrowing with skepticism when Mr. Anderson went over the free trial.

"How much do we owe you for the belt?" she asked.

Mr. Anderson smiled. "No charge. It's included. And…" he said, looking around. He snatched up a package—a pristine white gi, neatly tucked and folded and wrapped in plastic. "You look like a medium. Here."

Levi accepted the package, staring at the gi. "Really?"

"Yes, sir." Mr. Anderson glanced at his mother. "Again, no charge. I think Levi is going to do well here."

Levi heard the other kids out on the mat, tumbling around, as Mr. Tabb chatted with parents. Inside the office, though, his mother was getting fidgety. She eyed the clock and took a breath. "Mr. Anderson, I love that my son has taken an interest in karate. To be honest, I've been a bit worried about him," she said with a quick glance at Levi. "But, I'm not sure all of this is in our budget at this time. Do you have a price guide, or..."

Mr. Anderson nodded politely. "Mrs...."

"It's Miss. Miss Rocco," his mother said, pulling her brace behind her purse, close to her chest.

"Miss Rocco, if I may. Let's not worry about money right now. If Levi sticks it out these next few weeks, and I think he will, we can sit down and work something out."

The office door opened. Mr. Tabb whistled as he walked past the desk. Levi's mom looked at him and smiled, but then the smile fell. "Okay, I just, I hate to get his hopes up on this and then he has to stop."

"Let's see how it goes." Mr. Anderson clapped Levi on the shoulder. "In the meantime, I'd like you to come out tomorrow night," he glanced up to Levi's mom. "If you can make it?"

"Is there class tomorrow?" Levi asked.

"Nope." Mr. Anderson shot him a devilish grin. "Tomorrow night is 'Fight Night.' And I think you should come see what it's all about."

CHAPTER FOUR

"Fight Night? I don't like the sound of that." Levi's mother tapped on the steering wheel as they waited on the red light at Crawford Road.

Levi was tapping too. His leg jackhammered away as he inspected the creased gi before him. "Please, Mom. I'll do anything. I mean, he invited me to come on my first day."

She looked him over. "I haven't seen you this worked up in a while. Or ever."

Levi set the gi on his lap and looked out the window. His mother's phone chirped, stealing his attention as they drove off. He remembered the arguing earlier, but when he craned his neck to have a peek inside his mother's purse, she pulled it away.

"Don't."

"Is it him?"

She shook her head. Levi wondered why his mother hadn't told him his father was out of jail. *If* he was out of jail. Levi looked at the brace on his mother's arm. He was out alright.

So be it. This was why he was in karate, so if his father ever tried anything again, he would be there to protect his mother.

They drove in silence until they pulled into their apartment complex and Levi blurted out, "How long has he been out?"

His mother exhaled as though the question was exhausting. "A few days. Knowing him, he'll be going back soon. If he hasn't gone back already."

Levi's relationship with his dad was strained at best. He usually saw him a few times a year. Christmas. He could remember a couple of Thanksgivings. Some birthdays. Whenever he came around, it almost always ended with yelling and fussing and sometimes, in his mother's case, worse. His father had a hair-trigger temper and was always on the hunt for an easy buck. A bad combination, which was why he'd spent the better part of Levi's life in jail.

At home, in his room, Levi unwrapped the gi and tried it on, smoothing out the folds. It was super white and plain, but it was better than basketball shorts. He practiced what he'd learned on the mat, though it was hard to cover defense techniques and grab holds on your own, so he mostly did kicks and what he could. Right side guard, left side guard. Backfist. Reverse punch. Splits. More Kicks.

He watched himself in the mirror. He would be ready for Fight Night.

Levi relayed every detail of karate class to Gina the next morning at the bus stop. At school he told her again, then one more time on the way home. Gina listened the best she could, even removing her earbuds as he rambled on during the bus ride home.

"So, this sparring thing. Are you going to get all beat up?" she asked.

"No, I mean, I don't think so." Somehow, this had never occurred to Levi.

Gina's nose wiggled as she wrinkled her brow. "Okay, but I mean, sparring, by definition, is fighting."

"Yeah, I know. Maybe I'll just watch. I'm not sure I'm even going yet. Mom hasn't said."

Gina smiled at Levi. "Well, maybe I could talk Heather into giving you a ride. I mean, if you need one?"

Levi's heart picked up a beat. "Really?"

Gina rolled her eyes and laughed. "Wow, you're so pathetic."

Levi turned away.

Gina nudged his shoulder. "What time?"

And that was how Levi ended up in the backseat of Heather's car, the music blaring and the wind screaming through the open windows as they cruised down Crawford Road at 5:45 that evening.

"Okay, dorks, I'll pick you up in an hour, right?" Heather said, throwing her hand behind her head to fix her hair as they came to a stop in the parking lot.

Gina glanced back at Levi. "Does an hour work? If it doesn't, let me know, Heather is kind of like our Uber today, so..."

Heather smacked her little sister's arm. "Don't push it, Genie."

Levi cleared his throat. "An hour works. Thanks, Heather."

"You're welcome, Levi. Go kick some a— uh, some butt. Okay?"

Levi met Heather's aqua-blue eyes in the mirror, and his whole body turned to jelly.

"Earth to Levi." Gina stood at the opened door, motioning for him to get out.

Levi shrugged. He felt kind of silly wearing the gi in front of

Heather, but it seemed she wasn't paying much attention, driving off just as soon as the door shut.

"You know my sister is in high school, right?"

"Yeah," Levi said, fiddling with his belt. His dingy shoes looked extra filthy in contrast with the new white of his karate pants.

Gina was still glaring at him. "And she has a boyfriend," she added.

Levi only stared at her blankly.

"Oh, just come on," Gina said, setting off toward Kick City.

It was only the second time Levi had ever walked through the doors of the karate studio, but almost immediately, he could tell everything was different. He bowed, kicked off his shoes, then noticed that none of the six or seven kids in the studio were wearing a gi.

Even Mr. Anderson, who sat in a chair joking with a student, was wearing only a Kick City Karate t-shirt. Levi's face went hot with embarrassment as he bowed. Meanwhile, Gina simply plopped down on the floor, her back against the wall. She noticed a pair of shoes next to her and wrinkled her nose. She scooted another foot to her left. Levi chuckled.

Sometimes Levi wished he could be more like his best friend. Nothing fazed her; she was all confidence.

Mr. Anderson called over to him. "Levi, my man. You made it."

Levi bowed onto the mat, his new gi stiff. The other kids, ranging in age from twelve to eighteen, maybe older, he guessed, nodded his way.

"So," Mr. Anderson got to his feet and clapped his hands. "A few things, sir. You don't need your gi at Fight Night. I should have mentioned it. So you can lose the top, got it?"

"Uh huh."

Mr. Anderson turned his head with a smile.

Levi corrected himself. "I mean, yes, sir."

"Nice. Okay, so tonight you will mostly observe. I know you won't know a lot of the kicks and techniques, but just fall in and do the best you can, all right?"

From her spot on the floor, Gina cleared her throat. "Um, sir?"

Mr. Anderson looked past Levi and noticed Gina. "Hello, welcome to Kick City."

Gina held up her phone. "Can I get the Wi-Fi password, or is that like, hush-hush?"

Mr. Anderson glanced at Levi, who could only shrug in his friend's defense. For the first time since Levi had met the man, Mr. Anderson looked like he didn't have all the answers. "Yeah, I can get that for you, hang on."

Mr. Tabb, over near the counter, pounced. "Would you like a free lesson?"

Gina's eyes widened. "No thanks. Um, sir. Not at all."

"She needs the Wi-Fi password," Mr. Anderson said.

Mr. Tabb hustled over to Gina. "It's KickCity."

Gina looked up from her phone, her mouth parting. She blinked once. "Seriously?"

Mr. Tabb and Mr. Anderson exchanged glances.

Gina entered the password then shook her head. "Okay, wow. Okay." She noticed they were still watching her. "I mean, thanks, sirs."

With a clap of his hands, Mr. Anderson got started, and it wasn't long before Levi was sweating as they warmed up. He did his best to keep pace as they practiced something called blitzing. He watched and copied and did what he could until Mr. Anderson corrected him.

A half an hour later Levi was huffing for breath. He was given some loaner equipment—helmet, gloves, chest guard, and foot pads that seemed a size too big—then paired up with Tony, a taller boy who looked like he was in high school.

Running through the combinations, Levi found that getting hit wasn't all that bad after all. In a way, it woke him up, and soon he was dishing out the blitz combinations as well. At one point he crouched, faked, then stutter-stepped before he took off. He threw a kick, then flew in, connecting with a backfist.

Tony staggered back, surprised.

Mr. Anderson stepped onto the mat. "Tony, you're going to let this kid come in and knock you around like that?"

After that, Tony hit Levi a bit harder, came at him a bit faster, and before Levi could land another punch, Mr. Anderson had them gathered at the black line.

He set up four orange cones as a makeshift ring. He explained point sparring to Levi and matched up some of the oldest kids first. They clashed, colliding with lightning-strike punches or kicks, and then it was over. Point this side. Point that side. It all happened so fast, Levi could hardly keep track of who was winning.

Levi wasn't ready—he didn't think he'd ever be ready—when Mr. Anderson called him into the ring. Tony stood before him, rolling his neck.

"Okay, touch gloves," Mr. Anderson said.

Levi held his glove out to Tony, who tapped it with his own.

Mr. Anderson looked at Levi. "Just do what you've learned, okay?"

"Come on, Levi!" Gina yelled from her place up front. Everyone in the room turned their head to her.

Mr. Anderson smiled, then instructed them to *fight*.

Before Levi could blink, Tony was all over him. Levi's head knocked back, and Mr. Anderson called the point for Tony.

"Bounce, Levi. Stay on your toes and react. Be ready. Got it?"

Levi nodded, and Mr. Anderson backed up. "Fight."

Tony came again. This time Levi knocked his kick away but when he went to counter Tony caught him in the face with a backfist.

"Point."

Two-zip, just like that. Mr. Anderson didn't say a word this time, just separated the two fighters and called them to the center. "Fight."

Bouncing on his feet, Levi decided he wasn't going to wait. He faked once, then came at his opponent with the flip kick he'd learned on the sidewalk. Surprisingly, Levi's foot connected with Tony's head.

"Point!"

The entire room let out a collective gasp. Someone called out, "What?"

Levi stood on the mat in stunned silence as he received his first ever point in sparring.

Tony shook it off and smacked his helmet. He bounced as he readied himself for the next round.

Mr. Anderson was grinning now. "Point, Levi. Better be ready, Tony."

The next clash was over in a second. Tony scored easily with a punch to Levi's chest. Just like that, Levi was back on the sidelines.

The other students smacked him on the head as the next fight started. "Dude, that kick!"

Are you really a white belt?

Where did you take karate?

Levi shrugged it off. He had lost 3-1, but the other students were acting like he'd just won the championship. Before he got another shot in the ring, Gina was up, and Heather's car sat parked outside.

Levi let Mr. Anderson know his ride was there. Mr. Tabb

took control of the sparring, and Mr. Anderson helped him take his gear off. "What'dya think?"

"I liked it," he said, quickly adding "sir" at the end. His head was slick with sweat and his heart was still sparring with his ribcage. He couldn't remember the last time he was so tired yet satisfied. And confident. He'd gotten in the ring, and it wasn't so bad. He could do this.

Mr. Anderson set a hand on his shoulder. "You don't mind getting hit, that's a big part of fighting." He stood in front of Levi and leaned down to look him in the eyes. "I'm going to tell you this once, okay? And I don't want you to let it go to your head. You got it, man. You have what it takes. But you need to work. A lot of work." He chuckled. "The good news is you have the tools to be great. Do you understand?"

Levi swelled with pride. Adults rarely noticed him at all, much less told him he could be great at anything. He nodded. "Yes, sir."

Mr. Anderson slapped him on the head. "Good work tonight. Next class is Saturday, think you can make it?"

"I'll be here."

"That's what I like to hear. And bring your friend."

"Oh, I don't think she wants to do karate."

"I don't," Gina said. "But I could definitely help you with marketing. You don't have much of a social media presence."

Mr. Anderson stared at Gina as though she were speaking a foreign language before he turned back to Levi, as though he could translate for his friend. Heather honked the horn again.

Levi said goodbye and bowed off the mat.

CHAPTER FIVE

Mr. Anderson replayed the kick over and over again in his mind. It was truly remarkable. The kid had taken roughly forty minutes of karate and scored a hook kick against one of his better sparrers. *Lucky*, Mr. Tabb had called it. But Mr. Anderson didn't think so.

First, the kid wasn't a wimp. Of course, Mr. Anderson never called his students names, but truthfully, a lot of the kids who came into the studio were soft. They played video games for hours and ate fast food and arrived on his mat pale or flabby and couldn't get through a round of jumping jacks without needing water or a rest. But this kid never needed anything. Maybe a little bit of praise to boost his confidence, but that was it.

The matchup with Tony had been a test. Mr. Anderson wanted to see how the kid would react to getting pummeled. He'd almost hoped the kid would get frustrated, rip off the helmet, and go sit against the wall and pout with his friend. He'd seen it too many times to count. And if the kid quit, Mr. Anderson could move on and focus on recruiting. It would save him the hassle of getting invested.

And he *was* invested. The kid was cool. He'd taken the hits, absorbed them like nutrients, and even had the wherewithal to blitz at the right moment.

Mr. Tabb was wrong about him being lucky. Mr. Anderson knew better. He saw the flashes of brilliance. Give him a year with this kid—classes, training seminars, Fight Nights—and, well, Mr. Anderson would be able to show him off at tournaments and trot him out at promo events, and they'd never have to worry about who was fifth in the state again. They'd never look at little old Maple Ridge the same way.

Four years of falling behind. Always last in revenue, new students, tournament placements. No, it wasn't why Mr. Anderson did what he did, but he couldn't ignore the obvious.

What got him out of bed each morning was the students. The pride on their faces when they achieved their goals. The confidence as they grew. When they finally broke that board or executed a move for the first time. It warmed him to see the smiles as he gave out accolades at the end of class. That was why he taught karate. To instill the confidence, the values, to help shape these kids into strong adults.

But he had to pay the bills. He had to win sometimes. He had to recruit and grow and continue to keep pace with the other studios. It was just part of the business.

Mr. Anderson smiled, thinking about the girl with the blue hair. He'd never get her on the mat. But that line about social media presence. These kids knew so much about computers and the internet. At twelve, Mr. Anderson was roaming the woods with a stick for a sword, trying to sneak up on squirrels. Now they were laughing at his Wi-Fi passwords. He'd have to change that, soon.

He set his keys in the bowl as he entered the house. In the living room, his wife cooed to their son.

"Daddy's home," she said, and Mr. Anderson stopped in the doorway. The baby wore a onesie that read, *Daddy's Favorite Ninja.*

The baby squealed. Mr. Anderson did his best to set aside all the worries of his day as he scooped up his son. "How are those kicks? Did you work on them?"

"He sure did," his wife said with a yawn.

Mr. Anderson bent down and kissed her. "Were you guys waiting up for me?"

The baby let out a whoop, and Mr. Anderson brought him to his chest as he sprawled out on the floor. "So that boy, the one I was telling you about yesterday? He came tonight."

"To Fight Night? Already?" She looked him over and smiled. "I'm guessing he did well?"

Mr. Anderson cocked his head.

His wife laughed. "You've got that look."

"What look?"

"The one you get when you're super excited about something. Which, is a lot, but still."

Mr. Anderson lay back with his son, holding him up. "Yeah, the kid is going to be good. Really good, I think."

"You mentioned his...situation. Any idea how he's going to pay for class?"

"Haven't gotten that far."

His wife shot him a lazy smile. "Oh, I think you have. I think you know."

Mr. Anderson sat up on one elbow. "I was thinking about extending his pass."

"Extending, huh? Based on?"

"A hunch."

Mrs. Anderson didn't say anything, which told him a whole lot.

"What?"

"You see something in this boy?"

"I do. I see a lot in him."

"Does it look familiar? Like maybe something you'd find in the mirror?"

CHAPTER SIX

Gina wasted no time launching into her plan at the bus stop on Friday. "So, I did some thinking."

Levi stopped in his tracks. Gina doing some thinking was never a good thing. The last time she "did some thinking" they ended up in Principal Ramos' office after Gina roped Levi into joining her protest (a human chain) of the school's decision to cut down a row of oak trees that lined the back tennis courts.

The bus arrived and Gina pocketed her phone. "I can get Kick City all set up. They need a new webpage. The one they have is complete garbage. Seriously, it looks like something my grandmother would have used in the nineties. They don't have a TikTok account, or Instagram. It's like they're not even trying."

Levi plopped down and gazed out the window, careful not to encourage his friend. He didn't want to make waves as a beginner. His plan was to go to Saturday class, but as of yet, he had no ride. His mother was working all day. He figured he could walk. If he left early enough, he could get there in a half hour. Probably.

Gina nudged him in the ribs. "Hey. Are you listening to me? The socials haven't been updated in months. And what is up with the merch? Did you see the sun-faded bags in the window? They need to step up their game."

"I think they care more about karate than all that stuff."

"Yeah, well, all *that stuff* gets people in the door. You know what, I'm going to use you as my demo. We'll shoot a video of you in your gi doing all your moves. I'll show it to them, and maybe they'll let you take some lessons for free. You're welcome, by the way."

Levi did his best to tame his friend's wild ideas, but it was impossible. Besides, "What moves? I've been to karate like twice. And one of those times wasn't even a lesson."

Gina smiled. "True, but you look cool in your gi, and you look like you know what you're doing. Probably why the dude asked you to come."

Levi turned to his friend. "Really?"

She shrugged, some color finding her cheeks before she set her head back and laughed. She took out her phone. "Yeah, I mean, I guess. What do I know? Anyway, I did find a couple of videos, from a few years ago. Is this your instructor dude?"

Gina held the phone out, and Levi leaned forward for a better look. The man on the screen looked like Mr. Anderson. His hair was a little longer and darker, but the way he moved was clear. It was him, no doubt, doing some kind of instructional video. Levi leaned closer to hear better.

If you want to fight like a superhero, you have to train like one. So it takes stretching like this... He plopped down to a split. *If you want to do this...*

The screen flashed and Mr. Anderson was on his feet. He planted, took a step, jumped into the air, and executed a crisp spinning hook kick.

"Nice, right?" Gina said, nudging Levi with her elbow. "There's another one too. Something called a tornado kick. Are you going to learn how to do that?"

Levi shrugged. "I don't know. Maybe? I hope so."

Levi sat with Gina and had her replay the video five times on the way to school. He studied the kicks until the bus stopped for good and kids shuffled to their feet, until Noah Harris bumped the seat, stopping the line exiting the bus, and looked back to Jeremiah Durham. "Aww, look at how their heads are touching. The two rejects are in love."

Gina jerked away and pocketed the phone. Levi straightened as Gina stood and regarded the two smirking boys. "Is that really the best you can do?"

Jeremiah was still laughing, but Noah's smile dropped and he sort of bumped his friend to get going.

Jeremiah didn't get the message. "Huh?"

Gina rolled her eyes. "Don't worry. They say there's someone for everyone out there. Even you, probably. Maybe." She bit her lip and shot him a sympathy stare. "Hmm. Hopefully."

"Whatever, freaks," Jeremiah said, and got moving.

School wasn't easy for Levi. He wasn't as quick or as confident as Gina. They had no classes together, as she was in mostly accelerated courses and he was in regular ones. He had a few other friends, or, acquaintances, but no one he really confided in. And while there were always going to be jerks like Noah and Jeremiah, he usually felt more invisible than anything else.

And if school was hard for Levi normally, it was near impossible after seeing those kicks. In science class, Levi was so engulfed in a daydream about the moves he'd seen Mr. Anderson doing that he didn't hear the clip-clop of Mr. Roy's loafers until it was too late. "Any ideas, Levi?"

Levi snapped out of his dream. Mr. Roy had been discussing something about wavelengths and the speeds at which they were traveling. But Levi had been replaying Mr. Anderson's tornado kick in his mind for the last twenty minutes, and it was all he could do to lift his head up and blink. "Huh?"

The class chuckled. Levi's face burned a hot crimson when Mr. Roy, a short, stocky man of around fifty, did that grimace-smile thing. "Very good, Levi. 'Huh' is a perfect description of the displacement."

Mr. Roy was an okay guy, but he'd call you out in a second if you weren't paying attention. Levi returned his gaze to his desk and kept his head down until Mr. Roy turned and clip-clopped back to the whiteboard.

"Try to stay with us, okay?"

So he tried. But his brain was fixed on karate and refused to take on any new ideas. He ran through sparring combinations in his mind, what he could try to do better the next time he faced Tony. He thought about class on Saturday and all the questions he wanted to ask Mr. Anderson and Mr. Tabb. And then there was Gina's stupid idea, to film him doing karate moves he hardly knew.

He wasn't so sure about that one. Probably a bad idea, posting videos for the world to see. He was barely even a white belt, the kids in the class would probably laugh him out of the studio.

It was only minutes after getting called out that his mind had drifted back to karate. Cooper, who sat beside him, elbowed Levi's arm. "Hey, man. Hey."

Cooper passed Levi a worksheet. It might as well have been written in code. He was going to have to get a grip.

That evening, Levi was alone at the apartment when the phone rang. He didn't recognize the number on the ancient landline but knew exactly who was on the other end once he picked it up.

"Hey, Levi."

"Oh, hey."

Levi's dad hacked and coughed into the phone. Music played in the background. The clinks of glasses and men talking.

"Mom's not here," he said, then regretted it.

"I called to speak to you. How are you, son?"

Few things bothered Levi as much as when his father called him *son*. A *son* was someone you tucked in at night, looked out for, provided for, took to baseball games, and taught how to build forts. At least that's the way Levi saw it.

"I'm good." Levi swallowed down the urge to say more. His father didn't deserve it.

"Good, huh. Look, I wanted to maybe pick you up this weekend, spend some time with you. How does that sound?"

Even if he wanted to see his dad, Levi would never, ever, allow himself to get his hopes up for that to happen. Sure, he fell for it the first ten or twenty times, but he'd learned his lesson the hard way, and any hope he had was buried under thick, pink scar tissue and would never resurface. And again, hanging out with the guy who'd hurt his mother didn't seem like all that great of a time, anyway. Still, Levi tread carefully. "I don't know, maybe."

His father laughed. Someone was talking nearby, laughing loud. Levi pictured his dad outside the bar. He remembered a few times with his mom when he'd wait in the car while his mom would chase him down. They'd go from bar to bar, looking for his dad's truck, then she'd run inside some low-slung building with dark windows and loud music. Usually, they'd come out shortly after that, his mother yelling about child support before he spent it all on drinking. Probably why she was wearing a brace on her wrist.

"You don't know, huh? Look," his father said, his voice deep and confident. "This thing with your mama. I don't know what she's telling you, but it was a misunderstanding."

Misunderstandings were mixing up orders at the restaurant. Misunderstandings didn't land you in the waiting room at the Med First Center. And the guy sure sounded guilty, bringing it up. Maybe it was because they were on the phone and not in person, or maybe Levi was simply tired of hearing excuses, either way, he blurted out a response before he could stop himself. "So, she just fell, huh?"

Had he really just said that? Usually his father's voice zapped him powerless. But now, after a taste of sparring, how he'd never felt the way he had when he was in the ring—where reaction time was all he had—Levi decided to put his fear to use.

"You got some mouth on you, kid."

Levi thought about Mr. Anderson, about grab defenses and sparring. He promised himself he'd be ready the next time his father tried to hurt his mom. He'd have to be. He'd react accordingly. "I guess so. Actually, I'm busy tomorrow anyway. I just remembered, I got karate classes."

"Karate?"

"Yep. Talk to you later. Bye, Dad."

He hung up the phone and practiced spinning hook kicks for the rest of the evening.

CHAPTER SEVEN

Traffic was light at 8:46 on Saturday morning as Levi set off for Kick City. He gave himself plenty of time to get to his ten o'clock class, with his gi safely tucked in his backpack, along with his white belt.

The sun was out, and the day was warming nicely, in the sixties already, as he let out a yawn that lasted several steps. He'd hardly slept last night, tossing and turning, the call with his father weighing heavy on his mind. Levi hadn't told his mother about it, not after her evening shift. He hadn't wanted to bother her. She was already worried about him hiking it all the way to karate, but her morning shift started at six, so there weren't any other options.

His stomach rumbled. He'd only eaten a few bites of a stale mini bagel, and he was regretting it as the gusts of fast-food breakfast hit him like a gut punch. He swallowed it down and plodded ahead, knowing it would be a long time before his next meal. He'd have to ignore it the best he could.

Levi misjudged the walk, arriving at Kick City, at 9:25, where he found Mr. Tabb fiddling with the keys as he approached the front door. Levi's feet slowed. He hardly recognized the instructor in street clothes, and he didn't want to seem too eager, but as he stood in the empty parking lot, he wasn't sure where else to go.

Mr. Tabb had just unlocked the door when Levi approached.

"Uh, hi, sir."

"Oh," Mr. Tabb said, turning around. "Good morning, Levi."

Mr. Tabb glanced over Levi's shoulder, out to the lot, probably for some sign of a parent.

"I walked," Levi said with a shrug. He looked down to the cracked sidewalk, the yellow paint peeling off the curb. He wiped the back of his neck.

"Oh?" Mr. Tabb said, then smiled. "Dedication. I like it." He nodded toward the door. "Right this way."

Levi looked around the dark studio as they went in. Mr. Tabb told him he could take a seat, and Levi plopped down where the parents sat as Mr. Tabb turned on the lights and disappeared to the back. With nothing but the sound of shuffling papers, the ding of a phone, Levi grew bored. He got to his feet and went looking around.

He studied the pictures of Mr. Anderson with students and other instructors. Trophies lined the front. Levi was leaning in, reading the largest trophy, when Mr. Anderson pulled into the lot.

Levi's chest tightened as Mr. Anderson jumped out of his truck and hurried for the studio. He always seemed so sure, so confident, even as he marched to the door. He entered with a bow, then stopped short. "Oh. Good morning, Levi."

Levi wondered if he'd done something wrong. He nodded toward the back. "Mr. Tabb is here. I was just..."

Mr. Anderson relaxed with a smile. "Going to get dressed? You brought your gi, didn't you?"

"Yes."

Mr. Anderson shot him a look.

"I mean, yes, sir."

"All right. Go back there and get ready. Then you can start stretching."

Levi followed Mr. Anderson to the back, where he'd spoken to his mother that day. Mr. Anderson pointed to the bathroom. "That way."

Levi hurried to get ready while Mr. Anderson and Mr. Tabb talked about an order and shipping costs. When he stepped out, Mr. Anderson smiled.

"Tell you what, we've got a few minutes before class. Besides, Saturdays are usually kind of light. Let's hit the mat and go over a few sparring combos."

Levi smiled, eager for some one-on-one time. Although he couldn't help noticing the way Mr. Tabb raised an eyebrow at Mr. Anderson.

On the mat, Mr. Anderson had Levi try another split. He went down as low as he could, and Mr. Anderson whistled. "And you've never stretched? Never worked on that before? Here, lean back. There."

Levi's legs burned. It was true, he'd never practiced. Certainly never tried a full split before. But he was motivated by the gleam in his instructor's eyes, just like the other day.

"Okay, up and at 'em."

Mr. Anderson had two pads, one wrapped around each hand. "Now, I want you to come in, high block, then reverse punch. Got it?"

"Reverse punch?"

His instructor called toward the back. "Mr. Tabb, can you come out here, sir?"

For the next fifteen minutes, Mr. Tabb and Mr. Anderson ran Levi through drill after drill. He did his best and picked up blitz techniques and how to rush through with his guard up and his fist ready to strike.

By the time the door opened and a young girl entered, Levi was choking down breaths, glistening with sweat.

Mr. Anderson bopped him on the head with the pad. "Great work. Now, are you ready for class?"

Levi nodded. "Ye—yes, sir."

"Good, go get some water. You have six minutes."

Mr. Anderson was right, Saturday was a light class. Only six other students showed up, and Emma was one of them. By the time Levi got a few sips of water, wiped his forehead, and his six minutes were up, he was brimming with energy, hopping on his feet, ready for whatever the instructor could throw at him next.

He couldn't help but admire the colorful belts on the students' gis. One green, one yellow, and two orange belts to go with the other two white belts in attendance.

They covered basic punches, did the grab defenses again (this time, Levi did not take Emma so lightly), and when they threw kicks, Mr. Anderson even called out Levi for his form.

Forty-five minutes went by in an instant. Levi was gathering his stuff when the sparrers showed up, rolling their necks and going through their bags of gear.

He had his gi off when Mr. Anderson found him. "You're not leaving, are you? I think you owe Tony a rematch."

Levi glanced over at Tony, who smiled broadly and motioned at him. "Bring it on, newbie."

Levi smiled back. It was just one of the things he liked about karate, how everyone was treated with respect, regardless of rank. Even the teasing was in good fun. He'd yet to run across any bullies, and it seemed everyone, including a white belt like himself, was welcome.

Before he knew it, Levi was strapping on his borrowed gear and standing in the ring. It wasn't Tony but Emma who stood before him, her head cocked and a hand on her hip. Again, even after she'd thumped him to the mat the other night, Levi couldn't imagine hitting her in the face.

Until she did it to him.

At the word *fight*, Levi's head snapped back as Emma blitzed him with a backfist. The students jumped in place and cheered.

"Point, Emma. Hey, Levi, did you come to fight today or what?" Mr. Anderson chided.

Levi shook it off. There was some chattering in the background as a few parents watched. Everything was more intense when it came to sparring.

Back in the middle of the ring, there was no time to waste. But then Levi caught something: Emma was smiling, elated with the point she'd scored, and Levi could tell it was coming again. She was already leaning forward on her toes, ready to spring.

"Fight."

As advertised, Emma came blitzing again. This time Levi easily dodged out of the way and countered with a backfist that landed on Emma's helmet.

"Point!"

The chatter in the room died down. One to one, and Emma was no longer smiling, unlike Mr. Anderson, who was beaming. He motioned for the two fighters to gather in the middle of the ring and go again.

Levi bounced on the balls of his feet like he'd seen the other fighters doing. With two classes and little training, he was going mostly on what he'd observed. Still, he knew enough to know Emma was not going to blitz again.

This time, Levi faked his own blitz. Emma reacted with her guard to her face, leaving her midsection wide open. Levi delivered a sidekick to her stomach for another point.

Some movement in the seats. The other sparrers edged closer to see what was happening. Things were quiet, and Levi hoped he hadn't done anything wrong. They lined up again, and Emma's face was tight, her eyes squinting as she hunkered forward. Levi already knew she was coming with everything she had.

"Fight."

Emma blitzed before the word was out of Mr. Anderson's mouth. Once again, Levi side-stepped her and landed a light punch to her head.

"Point, Levi. Touch gloves."

Levi kept his head down as they bumped gloves. He didn't want to seem cocky, and he couldn't trust himself not to smile at his first sparring win. Meanwhile, Emma ripped off her helmet. Her face was crimson, and she blew a wayward strand of hair from her eyes. Mr. Anderson told her to be ready to come back in, that she needed to focus on what she'd been working on. Emma took it in stride and said she'd be ready. But Levi noticed Mr. Anderson watching him closely. Had he done something wrong?

Mr. Anderson scanned the sparrers, then pointed to Tony. "Tony, in the ring."

Tony leaped into action. He fixed his glove, and Levi adjusted his padded boot. He wasn't sure exactly where the Velcro strap went, but he wrapped it around and quickly stuffed it to the side the best he could. When he stood, he was acutely aware of his status. He was only a beginner. But did that mean he was supposed to lose?

"Touch gloves," Mr. Anderson said evenly. The instructor was no longer smiling but almost frowning in concentration. Mr. Tabb had stepped out to watch as well. Emma, now standing with the other sparrers, looked on without expression. But to Levi, it seemed like everyone was rooting against him.

"Fight."

Levi fell back. Tony surprised him by doing the same. The older fighter circled Levi like a cat, toying with him, as Levi bounced, waiting, mirroring the other fighter around the mat. He had no idea what was coming or expected, only that this seemed like some kind of trap.

"Come on, Tony," a boy named Kevin yelled.

Tony cocked his leg up like he was going to kick. He flicked it once, and Levi jerked back.

A simple fake was all it took. As soon as Levi fell back, Tony was all over him. Two punches to the head as Levi ducked and dodged but ended up out of the ring.

"Point. Gotta stay in the ring, Lee."

Levi took notice of the nickname. He nodded, fiddling with the helmet that was too loose on his head as he returned to the center of the ring. Back in place, Mr. Anderson shot him a wink, and it was like a charge was set to his spine. Maybe he wasn't supposed to lose. Maybe everyone wasn't against him. He set his hands out, one at his chin, the other out in front. He bounced on the balls of his feet. The mat was like a bed of burning coals.

The other fighters were still calling out encouragement when Mr. Anderson brought his hand down. Levi didn't hear the *fight* to start the round, so he wasn't thinking but reacting when Tony closed in on him—smirking in the same way Noah and Jeremiah smirked at him on the bus. And when Tony happened to lower his guard, Levi shuffled up, cocked his leg, and threw three snapping kicks—one, two, three rat-a-tat kicks— to Tony's ribs before coming up with a nearly flawless jump spinning hook kick that knocked his opponent's helmet clean off his head.

Tony staggered back, out of the ring and nearly to the mat. He turned and glared at Levi, who could still feel the contact on his foot. Nothing was said. No "point," no "stop." Nothing.

Levi was only partially aware of his breaths or how at least two parents had jumped to their feet. Mr. Tabb's jaw hung open.

Mr. Anderson looked on with something between amazement and fury—like a teacher demanding to know why a student was cheating on a test.

Kevin spoke first. "Bro, what was that?"

Levi managed to shrug his shoulders. Tony stomped off to retrieve his helmet as Mr. Anderson finally called the point and had the two fighters line up. As Tony was fixing his helmet on his head, Mr. Anderson leaned in and said something to him. Levi couldn't hear much over the thumping of his heart in his ears.

Tony brought everything at Levi in the next round, and Levi found himself backtracking out of the ring with a warning. As inexperienced as he was, Levi still noticed his opponent was fighting with blind rage and not discipline. He was sloppy, looking to slug him rather than score.

When they lined up again, Tony faked a blitz then came in earnest. He stormed at Levi with a backfist. As with Emma, Levi was expecting it, and it seemed to come in slow motion. He knocked it away and lightly tapped Tony on his faceguard.

"Point," Mr. Anderson said flatly.

Levi waited for instruction, still trying to figure things out, when two hands found his chest and shoved him to the mat.

Levi sat up on his elbows.

Mr. Anderson stepped in and yanked Tony away. "What was that? You don't fight the sparrer after he beats you. You know that. Pull that stunt again, and I'll see to it you don't fight in another tournament."

Levi had never seen Mr. Anderson angry. He got to his feet, almost wishing he'd let Tony score instead of seeing Mr. Anderson call him out in front of the class.

Mr. Anderson clapped his hands. "Everyone on the black line."

Levi hurried to line up, and he couldn't be sure, but it seemed they made space for him. Emma seemed to be giving him more room.

Mr. Anderson paced in front of them. "Most of you know I run sparring a bit differently than regular class. I'm a bit tougher on you because I expect more from you. You are my fighters. But fighters or not, I always expect my students to carry themselves with respect and discipline. If you're not ready, you will lose. If you're not completely focused. You will lose." He stopped in front of Tony. "If you're not disciplined. You will lose.

"And losing is fine. We all lose from time to time. We can learn from it; it can help us get better." Again, he stopped in front of Tony. "But win or lose, we will always, *always* show respect. Am I clear?"

Tony nodded.

Mr. Anderson pointed to the mat. "One hundred pushups, sir."

Tony dropped to the floor.

Mr. Anderson made his way to Levi. "I need you to see me after class."

Levi swallowed down the lump of worry lodged in his throat. It seemed everyone was watching him. Here he was in his first week. And he was only here because of a coupon. He had no money to stay after the thirty days were up and no money to pay for his gi, and now he'd come in on a Saturday, showing off and making problems.

One week. And he'd already blown it.

CHAPTER EIGHT

After class, the students removed their gear and talked amongst each other as they packed up to leave. Tony stormed out of the studio without a word to anyone. A few kids had questions for Mr. Tabb. Nobody approached Mr. Anderson, not even the parents, as he sat like a stone near the back wall.

This was it. The end of the road. In the span of one class, he'd gone from new kid to outsider. He was folding his gi top when Emma walked over to him with her hand out.

"Nice match."

"Oh," he said, taking her hand. It was warm and soft, and it was hard to believe this was the same girl who'd fought him so ferociously. "Thanks."

She eyed the entrance. "Don't worry so much about Tony. He's just super competitive."

"I noticed," Levi said.

Emma laughed. "Well, I hope you keep coming to sparring. You're really, really good. Already."

"Oh, thanks. I hope so," he said, meaning he hoped to keep coming. He glanced over to Mr. Anderson.

"Where did you learn to do that kick, anyway?" Emma whispered, her eyes going wide.

"I don't know. In my room." He looked down.

Emma giggled as though Levi had told a joke. "Well, it was amazing. Okay, gotta go. Bye."

The studio cleared out. Emma grabbed her bag and was joined by a taller woman Levi assumed was her mother. They bowed, and a few other students made their way, and soon it was only Mr. Tabb, Mr. Anderson, and Levi.

It was quiet. Too quiet. The mat scrunched as Mr. Anderson got to his feet.

"Mr. Rocco," Mr. Anderson said, taking a glance at the floor-to-ceiling mirrors lining one side of the studio. Then he turned to Levi. "Let's talk about that kick combination."

Mr. Tabb smiled, but Levi didn't feel like smiling. He stood at attention, the way he'd only just learned to stand. But everything was all wrong. He'd done something terrible.

Mr. Anderson read his mind. "You're not in trouble, sir. Although, I would like you to be completely honest with me."

"Okay," Levi said, because he wasn't sure what else to say. "Sir."

Mr. Anderson stood before him, hand behind his back, staring Levi directly in the eyes. "Have you taken karate before?"

Levi shook his head. "No. No, sir."

Mr. Anderson held his gaze for five seconds before he started pacing again. "Nothing? Not one class or seminar? No karate camps or vacations?"

Levi had no idea there was such a thing as karate camp. He'd never been to a camp of any kind. And vacation? He went to the lake a few times last summer, but that was about it. "Uh, no. No, sir."

Mr. Anderson glanced over to Mr. Tabb. They seemed to be

having an unspoken conversation—maybe an argument—with their eyes.

Mr. Tabb spoke next. "It's fine if you have, Levi. Honestly. We just want to know what we're getting."

Know what we're getting? Levi was confused. He glanced from one instructor to the other. His shoulders drooped some. "I've only been here." Levi looked around. "Last week," he added, trying to clear things up.

"So, the kick?" Mr. Anderson said.

"The kick?"

Mr. Anderson nodded. "*The* kick."

Levi no longer felt like he was in a police interrogation, but more like he was in the principal's office. He'd only been honest with Mr. Anderson so far, so he figured he'd come clean. His shoulders fell some when he exhaled. This was going to be embarrassing. He closed his eyes and took a deep breath. "My friend, Gina, the one who came with me the other day—she wants to help you with social media presence," Levi said, talking fast, nervous, unsure what he was even saying.

"Okay," the instructor said, eyebrows up.

Mr. Tabb walked over and stood next to Mr. Anderson. They both looked confused.

Levi shook his head. "Sorry. Anyway, she found some videos. Older ones, maybe, on the site? You were doing those kicks, and—"

Levi flinched as Mr. Anderson jumped in place and clapped his hands. He turned and started poking Mr. Tabb. "I told you. I told you that was where he got it." He wheeled back to Levi. "Sorry. Sorry," he said, regaining composure.

"So, I'm really not in trouble?" Levi asked.

"Trouble? No," Mr. Anderson laughed. "Not at all." He smiled now, his eyes dancing. "So that's where you learned to do that kick? My videos?"

Levi nodded, then caught himself. "Yes, sir."

Mr. Tabb threw his hands up to clear the air. "Whoa, whoa, hang on. You saw Mr. Anderson do some kicks, *online*, and then just decided you'd try it in sparring, against one of our tournament guys? That's what you're telling me?"

"Well, I practiced it last night."

Mr. Anderson hung on Mr. Tabb's shoulder as both men fought off the giggles. But the air in the room seemed lighter now, and for the first time since class, Levi allowed himself to smile.

"Amazing," Mr. Anderson said. He reached out and set his hand on Levi's shoulder. "Welcome to sparring, Mr. Rocco. We're going to get you signed up for our next tournament in June."

Mr. Tabb looked like he wanted to say something.

Levi pointed out the obvious. "Um, sir?"

"Yeah."

"I don't, well... My free pass is only for a month."

More glances were exchanged between the two men before Mr. Tabb sighed and stared off at the entrance.

Mr. Anderson turned back to Levi. "You let us handle that, okay?"

"He'll need gear," Mr. Tabb sang under his breath.

"I got it, okay?"

Levi looked from one instructor to the other. Could he really take karate for free? And what was all the talk about gear? Before he had a chance to ask questions and thank the two men, a truck pulled into the lot. Levi nearly fell to the mat.

Outside, his father parked the truck and took his time getting out. He stubbed out a cigarette, spat, then started for the karate studio.

CHAPTER NINE

The kid turned to stone. One minute they were laughing, still in shock over the spinning hook kick—the kid had thrown it better than any student Mr. Anderson had ever seen— and the next, he was stuck in place, the color in his face draining as though someone pulled the plug.

At first Mr. Anderson thought maybe it was a goof, but as he followed Levi's gaze out the windows, he noticed it had everything to do with the man approaching the door.

"Welcome to Kick City," Mr. Tabb said in his customary cheerful greeting as he entered.

The man, who needed a shave, coughed a few times then snorted before he spotted Levi and settled back on his heels.

"Well, look at you," he said with a toothy grin.

Over the years, Mr. Anderson had worked with all types of parents. Stepparents. Grandparents, aunts, uncles, foster parents. Overly protective parents, meddling parents, worrying parents, and the bully parents, as he liked to call them. Kids didn't choose who raised them, and Mr. Anderson had seen it all. Sometimes, things were downright dark at home, and seeing the effect this man had on Levi, the disdain in his eyes, Mr.

Anderson realized Levi and his mother had far more troubles than karate fees.

"Hi," Mr. Anderson said as he stepped forward, almost as a shield for the kid. It made sense to him then. The brace on Levi's mother's arm. The defensive way her eyes scanned a room. "I'm Cody Anderson, lead instructor here at Kick City."

The man ignored the greeting and stared past Mr. Anderson to the kid. "You know, I had to go to three karate places in town to find you."

"Well, you found me," the kid said.

Mr. Anderson almost had to turn to make sure it was Levi behind him. The kid's voice was deeper, his tone cold. His words dripped with resentment.

The man finally looked to Mr. Anderson. "Some way to treat your old man, isn't it?"

Mr. Anderson worked to keep the smile on his face. "How can we help you today?"

"Just here to pick up my son, that's all."

"I'm not going with you," Levi stated plainly.

Mr. Tabb and Mr. Anderson exchanged looks.

The man stepped onto the mat, his filthy boots leaving a trail of dirt. He shook his head. "That so?"

Mr. Anderson was about to intervene when the kid took a step back. "Yeah, it is. And don't go near Mom again."

The man smirked, glancing at the two instructors like he was deciding what to do next. "I thought we could spend some time together. It's been a while, Levi."

"Yeah, because you were in jail. Where you should go back."

The man chuckled. But it wasn't a friendly laugh. Mr. Anderson read the violence brimming in his eyes.

"Listen. I'll wait in the truck. Go get your things, and I'll give you a ride home. Maybe we can get some lunch." He glanced at Mr. Tabb, then to Mr. Anderson. "Nice place you got here."

Once the man was gone, the kid deflated before Mr. Anderson's eyes. Levi was fighting off the trembles in his hands as his chest rose and fell with empty, shaky breaths.

Mr. Anderson helped him to a seat and knelt beside him. "Just breathe. That's it. Take it easy. You're okay."

The kid dropped his head as though he were ashamed of himself. But Mr. Anderson wasn't judging. He knew all too well what it was like to panic. For your breaths to go racing off before you could catch up.

The door opened. Danielle Hudgins entered the studio with her father. Mr. Anderson had completely forgotten about his one-on-one session. Thankfully, Mr. Tabb chatted up Mr. Hudgins while Mr. Anderson got the kid to his feet and helped him find some privacy in the office.

Mr. Anderson got him situated in the back. The kid was a shell of the fighter who'd just thrown those amazing kicks on the mat. His breathing was short, rapid-fire wheezes. Mr. Anderson sat across from him. "Breathe, Levi, just..." He tried to get the kid's eyes. "Breathe through the nose, then exhale from your mouth. Good."

A few minutes later, the kid was staring at his feet. "I'm sorry. I'm really sorry. I didn't know he was coming."

"It's okay. So, you..." Again, Mr. Anderson had seen some things, lived through some things. And yet, he wasn't sure how to proceed. He was thinking of his own child, a little bundle in his wife's arms. How he couldn't wait to hold him when he got home that afternoon.

Then, Levi started talking. "He was in jail, but they keep letting him out."

Levi confirmed what Mr. Anderson had suspected. His mother had finally come clean, about how his father had tried to come into the apartment, but his mom wouldn't let him. How his dad yanked her by the arm, and she fell. How it wasn't the first time his father had hurt her. How he'd even stood there and watched it happen before.

"It was why...why I wanted to learn to fight, really."

"You want to defend your mom?" Mr. Anderson asked. "That's why you wanted to take karate lessons?"

The kid wiped his face, nodded. "Yeah."

It stole his own breath to think about it. "Levi, look at me," he said gently. "Listen, okay?"

Mr. Anderson scooted closer. He'd had so many conversations in this tiny room that was full of weapons and storage and motivational posters. He'd recruited in this room. He'd talked kids out of quitting karate. He'd looked parents and children in the eyes and promised to always have their best interests in mind. And he'd always meant it. But this time it was different. This time he was talking to another version of himself.

"We can't control what happens out there. Okay? Adults make decisions. Bad ones, good ones, and in between ones. But none of that is your fault. None. What you have in here," he said, tapping at his own chest, "is yours. It's special. It's rare. And I promise you, I will do what I can to protect that."

The kid looked up. His wide eyes brimmed with tears and confusion. And Mr. Anderson was surprised by himself, making this promise to a kid he'd only known for a week. And while he couldn't explain why or put it in words, he meant what he was saying. Meant it with everything he had. He focused on Levi.

"As far as karate. We will teach you how to defend yourself. You've already got a gift, I see it. But you can't let that gift turn to hatred. Got it?"

The kid nodded.

Mr. Anderson pointed toward the door. "No matter what happens out there, I want you to protect your heart. Don't let anyone tell you what you can't do. And don't let anyone turn you cold."

The kid nodded again. He wiped his eyes. His gaze was more focused now, some of that confidence from the mat returning.

"Now," Mr. Anderson said, rubbing his knees. He knew he shouldn't meddle. Maybe he already had. But the way the kid froze up on the mat after seeing his father, what he'd just said. Mr. Anderson couldn't let that boy get in the truck. "You don't have to go with him. We'll call your mom and work this out."

The kid almost smiled. "Okay. Thanks, Mr. Anderson."

CHAPTER TEN

Mr. Tabb was still working with a green belt out on the floor when Mr. Anderson and Levi exited the office. Mr. Anderson called out to the girl, who looked to be struggling with a bo staff.

"That's it, Danielle. Keep your left foot out a bit more. I'll be right back and we'll work on that."

A quick greeting to the girl's father before Mr. Anderson instructed Levi to stay in the studio and sit near the back, against the wall. Bowing off the mat, Mr. Anderson exited the studio. Danielle, bo staff in hand, watched on as Mr. Anderson, still barefoot, approached Levi's father's truck.

From the window, Levi's breath caught as the scene unfolded in the parking lot. His dad turned as Mr. Anderson approached the driver's side window of the truck. They had a brief conversation, Levi's dad shaking his head the way he did when he was angry or felt slighted. But Mr. Anderson stood straight and composed as they spoke, and after a while his dad set the truck in gear and peeled out of the lot.

Mr. Anderson didn't show any expression as he walked back in. He waved Levi over. "Do you need a ride home today?"

"I can walk," Levi said. He had already caused enough trouble.

"Don't be silly. I can take you." Mr. Anderson looked back, then to Levi again. "Is your mom waiting for you?"

Levi, who'd already come clean, shook his head. "No, she's working."

Mr. Anderson took this in with a breath. "Okay, how about you stick around for a bit today, help us out?"

Levi couldn't contain his excitement. "Sure."

Mr. Anderson cocked his head.

Levi chuckled. "Sure, sir."

He spent most of the morning scrubbing the mats. Then he assisted Mr. Tabb with organizing the storage room while Mr. Anderson finished up another one-on-one session with a brown belt named Jamal. He emptied the trash in the office, then the bathroom, before the black belts arrived and did their own special training. It was going on three o'clock by the time Levi had cleaned the front windows, and Mr. Anderson grabbed his keys and asked if he was ready.

Truthfully, Levi was fine with sticking around and doing chores all day. But Mr. Anderson offered to get him a bite to eat on the way, and that was that.

Levi didn't hear from his dad again on Saturday. He spent Sunday working on sparring techniques in his room and spending a little too much time practicing the tornado kick. He watched TV with his mom.

On Monday, he found Gina at the bus stop. She was sitting on a fence rail and leaped up when she saw him. "Hey, how was karate?"

"Good. Really good." He eyed her skeptically. She was definitely up to something.

"Great. Okay, let's get started."

Before he could ask what they were starting, Gina was

setting up plastic bottles. She placed one on a fire hydrant. Another on a fence post. Then, stretching out on her tip toes, she sat one on a tree limb nearly as high as his head.

She stood back and looked it over. "Okay, this should work, right?"

Levi only stared at her.

She held up her phone. "Hello, the video, remember? I need you to kick the bottles. Shortest to highest."

"Kick the bottles?"

"That's what I said. Okay, get warmed up or whatever." She glanced down the street. "Maybe pull your hood up. And hurry, we don't have much time."

Levi yanked his hood up the way Gina suggested. He did some stretches and tried to tell her about the sparring sessions and what Mr. Anderson said about the tournaments, but she was too distracted on the bottle placement and her phone. When he asked if she was listening, she shushed him. Levi did as she said, mostly because he always did what Gina said. She was one of the few people Levi trusted in his life. His mom, Gina, and now, maybe, sort of, Mr. Anderson.

Gina back-pedaled, holding up the phone, and told him to do one of those "spinny kick thingies."

On the first try, Levi missed the bottle in the tree and fell flat on his butt.

Gina covered her laugh, then talked him into trying it again. Wiping his backside, Levi kept an eye out for the bus, *hoping* for the bus, until Gina got after him again. "Stop stalling. Kick it."

On the next try, Levi took a breath and tried to forget about the phone or where he was and what he was doing. He focused on what Mr. Anderson had taught him. The videos. He took a deep breath, cleared his mind, and went to work.

The bus was grumbling up the hill as Levi spun, threw the kick, and sent the bottle off the hydrant and into the grass.

When he turned around, Gina nodded to the fence. "Now that one. Go!"

Levi pounced, timing his jump as he leaped, swung the kick around, and nailed the bottle dead center. He landed in stance, his guard up.

Gina popped up from the phone, her eyes wide. "Yeah. One more," she said. "Go!"

In a blur, Levi did as he was told. Without thinking on it too much, he turned, planted, then leaped. The last bottle went flying from the tree branch as he landed perfectly in his stance. He dropped his fists and turned to Gina. "Was that what you wanted?"

Eyes round, Gina's open mouth spread into a smile. She shook her head. "No. I mean yes. It was perfect."

They climbed on the bus, taking their normal seats as Gina went to work on her phone. She swiped and typed, shushing Levi whenever he leaned over and asked what she was doing.

They were almost at school when she came up for air. "Okay, it's ready."

She motioned for Levi to sit next to her, and he slid in. She turned the phone to him, already posted and tagged for Kick City.

Gina had put some sort of grainy filter on the video and added what sounded like tribal music in the background along with subtitles.

Ready to become a warrior?

And there was Levi, although it was hard to believe it was him. His hood up, his fists clenched, his body crouched in position as he bounced on his toes. His movements were precise and decided. He deftly knocked off the first bottle on the fire hydrant before he turned and moved for the second bottle on the fence post. A quick hook kick took it out before finally, with two steps, he planted then leaped into a jump spinning hook kick.

He was still staring at the screen when it went blank.

Gina sat back proudly. "See, that's what I mean about advertising."

"How did you do that?"

"Shouldn't I be asking you that? You've been to, like, two karate classes and you look like Spiderman."

"Can I watch it again?"

She was still smiling at him when the bus stopped and Noah and Jeremiah made their way past them.

Jeremiah scoffed. "Look, it's the freak couple."

"Probably have freak kids," Noah added.

Gina was up in an instant. She pocketed her phone. "Wow, I'm so proud of you two. You're putting together complete sentences. Well," she frowned at Noah. "Almost. But keep trying."

"Whatever."

They started for the exit, but Gina couldn't leave it alone. "Oh, and at least our kids will be original. I mean, bullying in 2024? Kind of tired, you know?"

Levi stood, trying not to blush at the *our kids* comment. But he was mostly still thinking about the video as Noah shoved Jeremiah ahead.

"You posted that video?" he asked Gina.

She nudged his arm. "Sure did. You can thank me later."

Off the bus, Levi quaked with energy. His heart thumped along, his blood rushing through his veins. He smiled despite the bullies on the bus, wondering what Mr. Anderson would think about the video.

He didn't have to wait long.

Gina caught up with him at lunch. "So, our little video is a hit."

Levi wasn't sure what to say. He pointed out the obvious. "You're not supposed to be on your phone."

Gina rolled her eyes. "Okay, *Townsend*," she said, referring to Mrs. Townsend, the school principal. Then she turned the phone and tapped the screen.

Managing a quick glance around, Levi leaned in. He noticed the video had already amassed nearly a hundred hits. Gina tapped the screen again. "See? Kick City has already shared it."

"Really?"

"Yes, *really*. Look."

She navigated to the Kick City Facebook page. And there was Levi, kicking the bottle. Comments varied, from fire emojis to *who is that?* to *sign me up!*

"Wow.

"Yeah, wow."

Levi sat back and smiled. "Do, um, do you think Heather saw it?"

Gina's smile fell. She closed her eyes and laughed. "Yes, Levi. I'm sure she saw it and thought it was amazing. Anyway, for the next video, I was thinking we could do something here, at the school."

"Yeah. Wait, next video?"

"Yes, superstar."

That afternoon on the bus, Noah and Jeremiah kept to themselves as they passed Levi's seat. When he got home, he grabbed a quick snack, then got dressed. He practiced kicks as he waited for his mom to arrive home and take him to karate class.

He stretched, went over some sparring combinations. He tried to go through the defense grabs, but it was hard to do without a partner. Finally, at 5:48, his mother walked through the door.

Levi rushed toward her. "Mom, Karate starts at six."

She set her bags on the floor. She closed her eyes and took a breath. "I can't, Levi. Not tonight. I'm tired, and besides, there's no gas in the car."

A punch to the gut. All day long Levi had looked forward to karate. Between class and all the excitement over the video, it had kept him going when he struggled in science, then math, and as he ate lunch. He told himself that the day would end with him in the studio, doing what he loved. He should've walked.

His mom touched his cheek. "I'm sorry, Levi. I'm doing the best I can."

"I know." Levi nodded, turning away.

His mom set her hand on his head. She smelled like food and a hint of her vanilla lotion. "When is the next one?"

He glanced at the take-out boxes, trying to guess what they were having for dinner. A whiff of something spicy. Tacos, enchiladas. "Well, Fight Night is tomorrow, then class again on Wednesday, so..." Levi remembered what Mr. Anderson had said about fighting. The tournaments. Now he wasn't even coming to class.

On top of that, he was overcome with guilt. Thinking of himself when his mother was doing everything she could. And he hadn't even told her about Saturday. Or the amazing news about the tournaments. Or how his dad had shown up. She was always so tired; he wasn't sure where to start.

He changed out of his gi and did his best not to sulk while his mom shuffled around in the kitchen with the dishes.

"Dinner's ready," she said with a smile when he returned. Sure enough, it was tacos.

She was still in her work clothes, only now her hair was down and her shoes were off. But she still looked exhausted, so much it made Levi feel bad for talking about himself.

He took out two glasses, poured some ice water, and they sat down at the table. They may not have much, and homemade meals were rare, but leftovers weren't the worst thing in the world, especially tacos, and he was sitting across the table with the person he trusted more than anyone in the world.

"How was your day? I've been so busy, I haven't had a chance to talk to you."

"Good," he said, then, "Oh, so Gina made me do this video, for karate. Here, I'll get your phone and show you."

His mom waved her fork at him. "Nope, after. No phones at the dinner table."

"Phone, singular, you mean. I don't have one, remember?"

"Of course I remember. You remind me constantly."

Levi fell back in his chair and stared ahead. He wouldn't mention how he was the only kid in middle school without a phone. Even when it wouldn't cost any more than the antique landline his mother insisted on keeping around for when Levi was by himself. What good would bringing it up do, anyway? She'd just say no like she always did.

They ate in silence for a while, and Levi's only thoughts were about all the kids in karate class, practicing right that moment. Warming up, doing pushups and sit-ups and stretches. He'd need to do those after dinner, in his room. Work on those kicks some more too.

"So, homework?" his mom asked finally.

"I'll do it after we eat."

She cocked her head. "Levi, you don't have to be so miserable."

"I wouldn't be so miserable if I was at karate," Levi grumbled. So much for not sulking.

The fork came down again, clinking against the plate. Levi looked up. His mother didn't seem so much angry as defeated. She wiped her hair back and stared off somewhere, at the wall behind him. "I'm sorry. I do everything I can to provide for you. I work all the time. I don't enjoy it, Levi. Waiting tables, is that what you think I grew up wanting to do?"

Levi shook his head. "No."

This was why he never got a chance to really talk to her. Because it always turned into an argument. Or his mom would sigh and say how tired she was.

Sure enough, the sigh came from his mother. "No. It's not. I'm happy you've found something. I truly am. And I will take you tomorrow, and the day after." She reached out across the table. The brace on her hand was bulky and heavy, somewhat grimy now with bits and pieces of thread caught in the Velcro. "But after this free trial thing, I don't know how we can—"

Levi pounced, remembering the good news. "Mr. Anderson wants me to fight in a tournament. He said he'd take care of class."

His mother's face wrinkled in confusion. "Take care of it? How?"

Levi abandoned his tacos. "It's what he told me. I can go for free. He said it on Saturday. I never had a chance to tell you."

He spilled the story, everything, gushing about the match with Emma, then Tony. How Mr. Anderson made him swear he'd never taken karate lessons. But before he could get to the chores and the free lessons, he let it slip about his dad, and from there everything took a sharp turn downhill.

Levi's mother set her hand up to stop him. Her face went as red as the tomatoes on her plate. "He showed up there, at the karate studio?"

"Yeah, well, he called on Friday, then he showed up. But I told him I wasn't going anywhere with him. Then Mr. Anderson took care of it."

His mother shook her head. She looked like she was fending off mosquitoes. "He what?"

Levi shrugged. It was hard to put the feelings into words. The connection he and Mr. Anderson seemed to have. How the man looked at him in a way no one had ever looked at him before, as though he believed Levi was capable of things. For Levi, who'd gone unnoticed for so long he'd begun to suspect he really was invisible, being seen by Mr. Anderson had been like stepping out of the shadows and into the warm, broad sunlight. And when Levi was sparring, he believed in himself.

Before he could say anything to stop her, his mother was on the phone, at the dinner table no less, calling his father.

And then the yelling began.

CHAPTER ELEVEN

L evi slammed the car door and hurried for Kick City, leaping the curb, before tossing a wave over his shoulder to his mother. He collected himself, taking a minute to breathe, then opened the door.

It was Fight Night, and Levi had been pumped since school. Now he was jittery, ready to jump out of his own skin. But this time he was prepared, in his white gi pants and t-shirt. He bowed, then took notice of the room.

Presently, Emma was doing some sort of dance karate form to music. And whatever her problems with sparring, she was flawless here. She spun, kicked, threw crisp combination punches to the beat. When it ended, she jumped, bowed, then snapped to attention, beaming with a wide smile on her face.

Mr. Anderson applauded. "Excellent work, Em."

Tony was sitting with another boy, and they were laughing at something on his phone. A few new faces, kids he hadn't seen before, lined up already, pulling on their arms and stretching out.

"Mr. Rocco," Mr. Anderson called to Levi. He wore a

sleeveless Kick City shirt and black pants. "How are you, young man?"

Levi had been expecting Mr. Anderson to ask where he'd been last night. Instead, he only smiled. Levi's gaze fell to his feet. "I'm good, sir."

"Nice work with the video. Seems to have really taken off."

Tony glanced up. Levi couldn't tell from across the room, but it looked like he was fighting off an eye roll.

Emma wiped her forehead with a towel. She smiled. "Oh my gosh. It was so cool."

Tony snickered.

"Take a few more minutes and we'll get started," Mr. Anderson called to the room. He motioned to Levi. "Here, come back with me." He nodded toward the back. "Got something for you."

Levi tried to mask his surprise as he followed the instructor across the mat. Tony and his friend watched closely as he stepped into the office.

"Got your gear," Mr. Anderson said with a clap of his hands.

"Oh," Levi said, unsure how else to respond.

Mr. Anderson laughed. He looked through some bags then turned back to Levi, and he lowered his voice. "Everything good?"

"Yes. Yes, sir."

Mr. Anderson handed him a white trash bag filled with pads and weapons. Padded nun chucks, and some other stuff that Levi would try to figure out later. He swallowed hard, clutching the bag and staring at its contents.

"We'll need to get you a vinyl bag, none are in stock at the moment."

Still, Levi only stared.

Mr. Anderson lowered his gaze. This time when he spoke,

his voice was nearly a whisper. "If you're worried about money, quit it. I told you, we'll work this thing out. For now, I want you to walk out on that mat like you belong there, because you do."

Levi closed his eyes and nodded, doing his best to hold his lip from quivering.

Mr. Anderson set a hand on his shoulder. "Look at me."

Levi did as he was told.

"You deserve this. You belong out there. Now get yourself together and prepare to get knocked around. I have a feeling Tony has it out for you tonight."

Levi smiled.

Mr. Anderson shot him a wink and patted him on the back. "That's it. Now come on."

He thanked Mr. Anderson and took the bag out to the floor. He found a spot against the wall and hurried to get the gear on, struggling with the straps.

Emma arrived to help. "Those go around the ankle, then stick right there," she said, tossing back her hair then pointing to show him how the padded bootstraps fit. "It's a lot at first, and I didn't get a bag either, so my dad gave me this luggage case." She nodded to a sporty bag with wheels. It looked big enough to fit inside.

"Thanks," he managed.

"No problem," she said, with a smile. "Seriously, that video is amazing."

Levi wasn't sure what to say.

Emma stood up and set her helmet on top of her head. "Don't pummel me tonight, okay?"

Levi promised he wouldn't pummel her, although, then again, he knew Emma was capable of pummeling him just as well.

Soon, Mr. Anderson was calling everyone to the black line. Levi held his helmet, trying to get comfortable in the thick white pads, still stiff and shining. He noticed the other sparrers had mouth pieces, and he made a mental note to get one as well.

"Big group tonight. That's good. It's what I like to see."

Levi was about halfway down the line, although it wasn't shortest to tallest like at class. Sparring was different, less contained, and Levi sort of liked how it was everyone for themselves.

They did some warmup techniques, and Levi caught on quickly. Mr. Anderson helped with where to place his feet, and as he shuffled, blitzed, and attacked the body in the mirror, he started to feel more and more comfortable in his padded gear.

That was another thing about sparring. Here, he wasn't regular Levi, the kid in worn clothes. In his gear, he looked like everyone else on the mat. But he could stand out in other ways. He could throw his kicks harder, his punches crisper. He could defend himself, dodge and weave like his life depended on it. And so he did.

At some point, Mr. Tabb emerged from the back. He stood in the front of the room, and Levi could tell he was watching closely, as though he wasn't convinced about something. Levi thought he could use some convincing.

"Okay, let's get started."

Again, the ring was made, four orange cones making a square. Two sparrers were called out. Levi missed their names, but it was clear they were experienced fighters. They clashed immediately, but one fighter—tall and lanky and draped in a silky blue outfit—was the top guy. He was a blur of kicks. The match didn't last long.

Mr. Anderson smiled at the rest of them. "Who's going to get a point on Diego tonight? Anyone?"

It didn't seem that way. Levi had never seen someone so quick and strong. He had the reach, and his kick seemed to stretch across the room. Diego took out Tony, then Emma, then two other challengers before Mr. Anderson called his name.

"Levi, what 'cha got?"

Diego bounced in place as Levi took his position in the ring. He was nearly a foot shorter than his opponent, but Mr. Anderson didn't seem to notice.

From the start, Levi knew he was sunk. Diego came at him with a flurry of powerful kicks. Two fakes before a foot knocked Levi's head. Shaking it off, Levi stood before Diego, who took his spot, ready to do it all over again.

"Keep your guard up, Levi," Emma offered.

Tony mocked her.

Mr. Anderson simply called them back. Again, Diego came at Levi with his leg up, poised to strike. Levi dodged the first kick then ducked another. He got turned around but managed to keep his hands up, which blocked the next three strikes.

As Levi slipped out to safety, another barrage came. Reading his opponent, Levi knew he had to act. He blocked yet another punch and in a desperate heave, managed to throw a backfist that connected with Diego's forehead.

Mr. Anderson jumped between the two fighters and threw one hand Levi's way. "Point."

"No way. I got him first!" Diego cried out. He turned to the other sparrers, who stood on the line, stunned into silence and without expression, arms dangling at their waists. "I got him," Diego said again.

"Diego got him," Tony offered.

"I don't know," Emma said, her eyes wide. "It was close."

Mr. Anderson looked to Mr. Tabb, still standing near the front, although he'd edged closer onto the mat. "What do you say, Mr. Tabb?"

"It was close...but, I think you called it correctly."

Diego shook his head. But he was an experienced fighter,

more levelheaded than Tony. Diego kept his composure during a fight.

They lined up again. Diego came in a flash, like lightning striking a pole.

"Point, Diego."

Again.

"Point, Diego."

And then it was over.

As Levi took his place back on the line, Emma leaned her helmet close to his.

"You scored a point on Diego."

Levi nodded. "Yeah?"

"He was southern regional champion last year."

Levi looked at Diego again, annihilating his next opponent.

"Yeah, but I lost."

Emma raised her eyebrows. "Well, of course you lost," she said incredulously. "I mean, you just started karate. But no one gets a *point* on Diego Martinez." She shook her head just as her name was called to get in the ring. "You might be really good at this."

CHAPTER TWELVE

Mr. Anderson turned the key, locking the door. "Wait until he knows what he's doing."

Mr. Tabb pulled on the brim of his hat. "Just so you know, I didn't really see if he scored that point tonight. I was all the way across the room."

"But you had my back," Mr. Anderson said. "Which is why I keep you around."

Mr. Tabb chuckled. "If you say so."

"I thought he needed a boost of confidence."

Mr. Tabb stopped walking. "So you gave him that point?"

Mr. Anderson shrugged. He'd always been honest with Mr. Tabb. "It was too close to call. But just like the kid needs confidence, Diego needs to be humbled at times. It's good for him."

"Let me get this straight. You're making calls against your best sparrer, possibly the best sparrer we'll ever have—one who represents Kick City all over the country—for some project of yours? A kid we've had in class twice?"

"Diego is amazing. We all know that. Trust me, Diego knows all too well how amazing he is. But he's outgrowing us.

He'll leave for college soon. Besides, this kid, he could be *better* than Diego."

Mr. Tabb stopped twirling his keys. "Okay, now I've officially heard it all. I'm going home. Please, sir, get some sleep tonight. And stop referring to him as 'the kid' like he's some kind of prodigy."

Mr. Anderson's smile only broadened.

Mr. Tabb shook it off. "Yeah, goodnight." Mr. Tabb walked to his car and opened the door.

But Mr. Anderson was feeling giddy, hopeful, though he couldn't say why. "This kid is going to be something, I'm telling you. Mark my words." His words echoed out to the empty parking lot.

Mr. Tabb was laughing as he called back. "Consider them marked. Now, if you don't mind. I have some calls to make, recruiting to do. You know, paying customers."

"Good night, sir."

Mr. Tabb drove off, and Mr. Anderson was all set to get in his truck when the empty Kmart caught his eye. He studied it close, thinking of all that unused square footage and space. It would take some work, but standing there in the empty lot, he couldn't help but dream. He was still dreaming when he turned his gaze back to his little studio. A spark of inspiration hit. He jogged back to the building and unlocked the door.

Inside, he flipped on the lights, slipped off his shoes, and hit the mat for a hundred pushups.

Just like old times.

Mr. Anderson was still feeling ambitious on Saturday before class. He had a spark of energy he couldn't contain as the white, yellow, and orange belts lined up with four new kids in street clothes.

The new kids always wore the same expression. Eyes darting around, mouths closed to a tight line. They watched the others and did their best to mimic what they saw.

Then the kid walked in with his trash bag, and Mr. Anderson couldn't help but smile. While he knew he had to treat all kids equally, he couldn't suppress the relief that washed over him every time Levi returned.

Noting the way Levi bowed as he entered, Mr. Anderson read the kid's body language and confidence. He knew he'd done the right thing at Fight Night.

The kid took his place beside Emma, who quickly helped him tie his belt correctly. Mr. Anderson made a note of this, as well. Emma had obviously taken a shine to him.

"All right, come to attention," he called out.

Today they would be going over forms, a way of teaching basic movements and putting together skills learned in martial arts. The form they'd be covering today was Circle 3, part of the Eight Step Full Circle curriculum.

Mr. Anderson and Mr. Tabb lined the kids up and had them get into their fight stance. Mr. Anderson demonstrated the form, which involved several backfists and reverse punches before a barrage of kicks.

The kid picked it up instantly, like he had all along. Mr. Anderson wanted to know what Mr. Tabb thought of that, and so he called class to a halt.

"Everyone, watch Levi go through Circle Three."

The kid's face flushed. Sometimes, watching him train so intensely, it was easy to forget how shy Levi became in front of other kids.

Levi did his best to blink it off and took position. His voice was meek and small. Mr. Anderson knew that was something he could fix, though. What didn't need fixing, were his kicks.

"Circle Three," he stammered, then broke into a stance.

"Just breathe, Levi. And be confident, you got this."

The kid nodded, then set his feet. It was like he put everything out of his mind besides the task at hand.

"Circle Three!"

Mr. Anderson worked to keep his facial expression neutral as Levi executed the kata in perfect sequence. His punches were crisp—he could hear the snap of his sleeve with each punch. And the kicks. Oh, those kicks. High and tight and performed with black belt showmanship.

When the kid was done, the room broke into applause. Mr. Anderson exchanged a glance with Mr. Tabb, who cocked his head.

Class came to an end. Three out of the four new kids Mr. Tabb had brought in were never coming back. Mr. Anderson had a way of knowing these things—from their effort to their body language to a plain old gut feeling. The one kid, Danny, might return. He was around nine, fresh-faced and sweating, and Mr. Anderson was talking with Danny's father as Levi gathered his bag.

"Yes, I think Danny would make an excellent student here." He looked at Danny. "Did you have a good time?"

Danny nodded.

Levi happened to walk past, and Danny bounced on his toes, watching him like he was a star. "Dad. Dad, that's him!"

Danny's father nodded, then laughed. "We watched the promo video. A lot. The one with..." He nodded toward Levi. "That kid with the kicks."

"Oh, right. Hang on." Mr. Anderson hurried over to Levi. "Hey, Levi. Got a minute?"

The kid looked up and smiled. "Yeah, my mom isn't here yet."

"Oh yeah, about that. If you ever need a ride, I can pick you up. Starting Monday. No excuses. Got it?"

"Yes, sir," Levi said, the smile growing.

"Come help me out over here." Mr. Anderson led him across the room.

"Danny, this is Levi. Levi, Danny is thinking about joining us."

"Hey, Danny," Levi said with a smile.

"Can you teach me to kick like that?" Danny asked.

Levi glanced at Mr. Anderson, who cocked his head playfully.

"*I'll* be teaching you, Danny," he said with a grin.

Danny was still watching Levi as the kid backed off and found a place by the front counter to wait for his mother.

Danny's father looked him over, his voice lower. "That kid is only a white belt?"

Mr. Anderson nodded. "Well, he's moving to yellow belt today." He decided on the spot.

"Wow, and that was him in the video, doing those kicks?

"It is. It was. Although, he's somewhat of a natural. But yes, he's been coming for a week or two now." Mr. Anderson held back the urge to say that he was one in a million. He turned the conversation back to recruiting. "And what about you, Danny? Will you guys be back on Monday?"

Danny's father squeezed his son's shoulder. "I think so, yeah."

Beginner class cleared out. It was around eleven. The sun was out, and it was shaping up to be a good day.

And then came the call from Kenneth Keaton.

The black belts were warming up. Mr. Anderson stared at

the phone, almost wishing the call away. If karate was the balm that soothed his soul, Kenneth Keaton was the nagging splinter he could never get out of his thumb.

The son of his mentor, Kenneth was a few years older than Mr. Anderson but had never taken a karate class in his life—at least not that Mr. Anderson was aware of. He did the books, keeping close track of the accounting portion of the Kick City chain, and ran it without regard for anything other than the bottom line. Mr. Anderson loathed talking to him, although it was necessary every few weeks.

Knowing he'd need privacy, he held up his phone to Mr. Tabb then tucked away in the back office.

"Kenneth," he said by way of greeting.

"Hello, Cody, how are things in Maple Ridge?"

"Well, you know. Trying to teach class."

Mr. Anderson hated how Kenneth called during teaching hours. He knew the schedule; he just didn't care.

"Great. That's great. Hey, looking over the sheets here."

Never good, Kenneth looking over the sheets. Poring over the numbers never meant *great work, keep it up.* It always meant Maple Ridge was lagging behind the other studios.

"Looks like you guys only had two sign-ups last month. Is that correct?"

"I don't think so. In fact, I believe we just had a sign-up today."

"Well, good, good. But that's this month. Anyway. Something going on down there?"

It was Kenneth's father, Master Calvin Keaton, who had taken Mr. Anderson in and trained him free of charge at eleven years old. Now, Mr. Anderson was trying to pay it forward with Levi. Karate was a way of life, something to teach, not sell like Girl Scout cookies. But this was the path Mr. Anderson had chosen, and besides, he was good with people, great with kids and parents. He reminded himself he had a small child to provide for and that the numbers meant growth. Growth was needed if he wanted to continue teaching karate for a living.

Mr. Anderson took a breath to quit grinding his teeth. "No, just that time of year I suppose. We're working on a few things."

"Well, I saw the promo. Not bad. One of your new recruits?"

"Something like that."

"What's the name?"

"Levi Rocco."

Some typing on the other end. Mr. Anderson pictured Kenneth slumped over, the glare of a computer screen shining off his glasses. "Hmm, not showing him on the books. Looks like he's still on pass?"

Nothing about the spectacular kicks, only that he wasn't on the books. Mr. Anderson bit the inside of his cheek before speaking. "Yeah, I wanted to speak to you about that."

"And I'm showing some inventory out. Weapons, gear. The full package. And a gi, it appears."

Mr. Tabb had the black belts running through exercises. What Mr. Anderson would give to be out there at the moment. "It's taken care of."

"Okay, great. I know it sounds small, but first it's a gi, then more weapons. Soon it's two, then three, then the numbers are shot."

It was more than he could take. "Look, Kenneth. I'll have to call you back."

"Sure, but before you go, let me remind you that the Pine Bluff branch is expanding. We've had to move because recruitment is so high. You're still in that abandoned lot, and from what I'm showing, we're not even filling the floor."

"Kenneth. I have a class to teach."

"I understand. I'll be down soon, and we can get this worked out."

Mr. Anderson hung up the phone. He was ready to hit something and hit it hard. Sometimes it was nice to work in a karate studio.

CHAPTER THIRTEEN

Gina claimed not to know anything about karate, and Levi was beginning to believe her as they hiked to the park where she set up an obstacle course that included a trash can, a metal bench, and a tackle dummy from the football field.

Levi was instructed to leap over the trash can, "do some kicks," roll, hop up on the bench, "do more kicks," and then take out the tackle dummy.

So far, he'd tripped over the trash can, got a mysterious purple stain on his new gi, and managed to fall off the bench. Twice.

They shot it four more times. Gina said she could splice it together and make it work. Levi shrugged. He took off his gi top to better examine the stain and asked if they could please leave the park.

Gina laughed. "Yes, sure."

At Gina's house, she worked on the video while Levi fought through his homework. At some point, he mentioned the thing about his dad the other day, and Gina looked up.

"He came to Kick City?"

Levi nodded. Gina abandoned the phone and stared at him

until he looked away. Sometimes he wished he could shut his mouth.

"Hey," she said, her voice softer than usual. "I mean, are you okay?"

"Yeah, I'm fine. It was just... I don't know what he wants."

Gina lowered her head, her eyes a bit wider. "Well, I'd hope he wants to spend time with you."

Levi thought about his dad's face the other night. The way he sneered at Mr. Anderson. He brushed it off. "Whatever it is, it's not that."

Gina got back to her phone, then set it down again. "I don't know how to say this, but has your mom like, talked to anyone? Like police, or something?"

Levi really didn't want to have this discussion. Especially not in Gina's house, where her parents were always laughing and joking with each other, or even kissing each other, causing Heather and Gina to groan and complain about the PDA. "I don't think he'll do it again. And he's left her alone, lately."

Going to the police sounded serious, and scary, and Levi wanted the problem to go away, not get bigger. Gina was still staring at him. And it only made things worse that her voice had lost its usual sarcastic edge.

"Okay, but hey. If it happens again, you have to tell me, okay?"

Levi nodded. He wasn't used to Gina being so serious. And he didn't want her to feel sorry for him. He got back to his math book, regretting having brought it up at all. "Yeah, sure." He looked at the clock and started packing up his things. "Shoot, I have to go. Mr. Anderson is picking me up."

Mr. Anderson arrived at Levi's apartment at 5:15 to pick him up for the 5:30 class. Levi jumped in the truck and noticed two things. One, the truck was immaculately clean. Not a speck of dirt, the dashboard shined, and everything smelled like vanilla. Second, Mr. Anderson didn't have that happy gleam in his eyes. He looked almost agitated, even when he smiled and asked Levi how things were going.

"Good, I think. My friend made me do another video."

Mr. Anderson nodded. "Nice, that other one has like a thousand views. I think that's good. Definitely our best one yet. You don't look so excited though."

"Oh, no, it's fine," Levi said, then, worrying Mr. Anderson would take his mood as ungratefulness, he sat up straighter. "Sir."

They got going down the street. It was weird seeing Mr. Anderson in street clothes, not in the studio. He looked so different. Younger. But the silence was getting to him.

"Everything okay, sir?"

"Huh?" Mr. Anderson tapped the steering wheel. "Oh, yeah, just bills and stuff. You know."

Levi nodded as though he did know. The only thing he knew about bills was that his mom got too many of them and had to choose which ones to pay first. Thinking of his mom, he should've cleared it with her, riding with Mr. Anderson. And back to bills, hearing Mr. Anderson talk about money once again had him worrying about karate. Free lessons weren't going to pay those bills.

At the Crawford intersection, Mr. Anderson finally seemed to come out of his funk. "Seems like we're both off today. Nothing some karate can't solve though, right?"

Levi was still thinking about bills and karate when Mr. Anderson stopped the truck, facing the studio. "My turn again. You okay, at home and all?"

Levi wasn't sure how to answer that question. He sort of nodded and shrugged. "Yes, sir. Thanks again for picking me up."

As they parked, Mr. Anderson turned on the radio, nodding

his head to a song about fighting through the night. Soon he was singing so loudly Levi couldn't hold it back and busted out laughing. And they were both bobbing and laughing to the song when a BMW zoomed through the lot and came to a screeching halt alongside the curb. The license plate read KICK CTY.

The radio went silent. Mr. Anderson was not laughing now, not even close. "You've got to be kidding me," he groaned.

A short, dumpy man in a plaid shirt and gray pants stepped out of the BMW and marched inside the studio. Levi wasn't sure what to say or do so he sat in the seat next to Mr. Anderson, who shook his head and muttered a few choice words under his breath. Finally, he snatched the keys and opened the door. "Come on, Levi. Follow me."

Levi did as he was told. Mr. Anderson made a line for the studio, allowing for a swift, curt bow before stomping for the back. Levi bowed then took his place beside Emma.

"What's going on?" he asked, sensing the commotion. The eight or so students were whispering and glancing to the back office.

Emma looked left, then right. "The owner just walked in. He's back there."

"Oh, is that bad?" Levi asked, trying not to look as confused as he sounded. He'd assumed Mr. Anderson owned the studio. But it couldn't be anything good, not after the way Mr. Anderson had reacted.

Mr. Tabb left the front desk and had the students come to attention.

Class went well. Levi learned new grab hold defenses and was able to achieve a full split. But he couldn't shake the look on Mr. Anderson's face when they arrived. All through class Levi had kept one eye on the office door, wondering about this mysterious owner.

It wasn't until they were being dismissed that the office door opened and the man stalked out, Mr. Anderson following, looking somewhat better but still as though he'd rather be doing a million other things than the task at hand. At least he was dressed for karate now, in his customary black gi.

The man in the plaid shirt stopped and looked them over. He said something to Mr. Anderson, and Levi's chest tightened as they both looked his way.

Mr. Tabb was fielding after-class questions when the man, who was a bit hunched, as though the bags under his eyes were pulling him forward, nodded, then stormed off.

"Levi, can I see you for a second?" Mr. Anderson called to him.

Levi swallowed down the lump in his throat.

Emma, fixing her belt, shot Levi a smile. "Good luck."

Once again, Levi found himself in the back office. Mr. Anderson was rolling his neck and looked like he was about to go in the ring for a fight. But he smiled for Levi's benefit.

"Have a seat," he said.

Levi lowered himself into the worn office chair that was crammed against the wall. On the desk sat a framed photo of a younger Mr. Anderson with an older man.

Mr. Anderson followed his gaze. "That was Master Keaton," he said, nodding toward the picture. "A military guy, he was stationed all over the world. He did two tours of duty in Vietnam, and later, he took bits and pieces of everything he learned and formed what we do here now. He started this place from the ground up. It all began in an abandoned warehouse downtown. As the warehouse grew, Kick City was born. Now there are five chapters in the state."

"He passed away?" Levi asked, noticing the past tense.

Mr. Anderson nodded. "Yep, few years back. Anyway, that man taught me everything I know. He was more than a Master; he was like a father to me."

Levi nodded, wondering where all this was going.

Mr. Anderson smiled. "Anyway, that was his son, Kenneth. The guy you just saw."

"Oh."

"Yeah, *oh* is about right," he said with a mirthless laugh. "See, Master Keaton's son doesn't see things the same as his father. It's a long story." He sighed. Then the gleam returned to Mr. Anderson's eyes. "But, there is something. Something big, and it involves you. And we need to have a talk with your mom."

"If it's about the money," Levi said with a sigh. "I could work here maybe, clean the mats?"

"No, no, not that. Besides, it's illegal. I'm talking about the Kick City Invitational tournament, in Richmond."

Levi turned his head like a cocker spaniel.

Mr. Anderson laughed. "I want you to fight. And uh, no pressure, but I kind of need you to win. I'm betting on it, actually." Mr. Anderson turned over some papers. "Quite literally."

Betting on it. Like, *gambling? Gambling.* The words made Levi think of his dad, and his limbs went heavy. "What?"

"Can you start training tonight? Private lessons. We don't have much time."

Levi wasn't sure what was happening. The ride over had been up and down. Then Mr. Anderson saw that car and went to the back. Now Levi was in a tournament. Taking private lessons?

Before he could answer, Mr. Anderson pulled out a yellow belt. "Oh, and here. Congratulations. You've earned it."

Astonished, Levi looked at the belt in his hands. "Are you... Wow."

"No time for wow, kid. Let's go."

Levi called his mom to explain he was going to stay. He asked if she could pick him up at nine. She started in with all sorts of questions, but Mr. Anderson gestured for the phone and promised her he'd get Levi home. They could sort it all out when she had some time.

And then Levi took a class. And after class, he was still on the mat, alone, bouncing on the balls of his feet.

An hour later, Levi's left arm was jelly from throwing punches. His legs were rubber from the bouncing. Mr. Anderson wasn't smiling and didn't seem to be having much fun at all as he drilled Levi on fundamentals. As much as Levi loved karate, his body had shut down. The crisp yellow belt had lost its luster. He kept looking out the front, hoping to see another car. A bus. Anything to save him.

"Have a seat," Mr. Anderson said, and Levi nearly collapsed to the floor. He'd been on the mat for nearly two hours by then.

Mr. Anderson tossed him a water bottle, then paced the floor. "Here's what we have. The good news is that you have it all. Natural ability, an incredible kick, great instincts and reflexes, good intensity to your movements. But we have a lot of work to do. We have to make you a smarter fighter. That comes with experience. We don't have time for experience."

Levi sipped water and wiped his chin. "So what do we do about it?"

Mr. Anderson slipped on a helmet and went for the gloves. He shot Levi a smile. "Well, we've got to cram."

CHAPTER FOURTEEN

Mr. Anderson watched from his truck as the kid climbed the stairs and got inside his apartment. As he drove off, he gripped the wheel, wondering what he'd just done, betting on some kid off the street to win the invitational. It was Kenneth's smirk that had done him in, the way he always brought up Pine Bluff and how Maple Ridge was last in recruiting. His talk of how low the numbers were. It drove him mad.

Now he'd done it. He'd called the kid a phenom. But was he really? It was hard to tell. Sure, his kicks were phenomenal, but could he be a champion sparrer, in two short months? That was a lot to ask of anyone.

If the kid won, Kenneth would have to shut his mouth and cut a check for five grand to the Maple Ridge Kick City chapter. Mr. Anderson would proudly display the banner out front. It would give the school a boost and buy him some time with the recruiting mess.

But if the kid didn't win...

Mr. Anderson could always go to Mrs. Keaton—who actually did own the studio. Although she could only do so much. Kenneth was holding the purse and was only concerned with numbers and profit margins. Mr. Anderson didn't think Kenneth would drive him out completely, but he would certainly make his life miserable.

As he pulled into his driveway, Mr. Anderson rubbed his chin and smiled. While training, the kid had caught him once with a powerful pop. He looked out to the three-bedroom brick house. It wasn't a mansion, but the yard was groomed, and the house was tidy. He'd come from absolutely nothing. His own mother had worked at a dry cleaner and it was all she could do to keep the lights on in their single-wide trailer.

From the window, the lamp casting a warm glow in the living room, Mr. Anderson watched his wife and child rocking in the chair. Once again, he glanced upward and thanked God for all he had. A beautiful wife, healthy child, his own home, and a career he loved. He never let himself stray too far from his roots to forget what really mattered.

It worked. He walked into his home with a smile on his face. He leaned over and kissed his wife, then kissed the baby on the crown of his head.

His wife yawned. "You're late."

"Yeah, and tired."

She nodded. "We made pasta. Saved you some."

Mr. Anderson came around the chair and kneeled in front of his wife. "I love you."

Her eyes crinkled with her smile. "I love you too. What's going on?"

"Well, it's about the kid."

"*The* kid." She grinned.

"I was working with him after class."

"You know, I think it's a great thing you've taken a shine to this boy, but there is also this boy." She bowed her head to the bundle in her arms. "He could use you around here from time to time."

A painful jab. Mr. Anderson nodded. He and his wife had been together since high school, and he knew well enough to admit when he was in the wrong. "I know, Marissa. I'm sorry. And I will. I was thinking you guys could come to the studio. We could give this boy his first lesson."

She turned to the little bundle nuzzled in her arms, fast asleep. "Want to go crawl around on the mats?"

Mr. Anderson stood and wiped his hair back. "Kenneth came to see me today."

Her face tightened. "Oh, why didn't you start with that? I could tell something had you worked up."

"Really?"

"Yeah, it's how you walk, with your shoulders all like this." Marissa lifted her shoulders, rolling them forward. The baby stirred.

Mr. Anderson laughed. "He's talking about the numbers again. Guess who's in last place?"

"I thought you guys were doing okay, with the free passes and all?"

"Not okay enough, apparently. We sort of had it out in the back office."

Marissa sat up straighter. More stirring. All the joking gone. She studied him closely. "And?"

"And I lost it. I said some things maybe I shouldn't have said."

"Cody."

"I bet him the kid would win the invitational."

This time she shifted in her seat, narrowing her eyes. She started to say something then stopped and lowered her voice, but the words came out sharp. "You said *what* now? A bet? Why would you do that?"

Sore as he was, Mr. Anderson took a few steps, then turned. He always needed to be in motion. He could never sit still for long, he needed to chase his dreams, to capture all his thoughts and ideas and sort through the pile. It was easier when his legs were moving. And now, with his wife glaring at him, he knew it was time to come clean. "He can do it, Mar. I know he can."

"Are you talking about the Kick City Invitational? The big one with all five chapters? And this kid. Hang on, you bet that *some boy off the street*, the white belt, would win the invitational?"

"He's a yellow belt now, I bumped him up."

She was still staring. "Are you delusional?"

"Kenneth thinks so. So does Mr. Tabb." He laughed, then regretted it. He and Marissa didn't fight much, and it took a lot to get her this worked up, but she was there now, and laughing wasn't going to help him make amends. All he had to go on was a feeling that this boy—who showed up on his sidewalk and wowed him from the start—could do something extraordinary. Apparently, he was the only one with this feeling.

"Cody, it's one thing to take a liking to a kid. Seeing yourself in him and wanting to help. Even to have him take lessons for free, that's commendable. But betting your future on him, *our* future, to do something you can't possibly expect—"

Mr. Anderson dropped back down to one knee. He looked his wife straight in the eyes. "He can do it, Marissa. I promise you that. He can win."

Marissa searched his face. Then, after ten, twenty seconds of silence—only the baby's breath and the glow of the lamp between them—she blinked.

"Okay, I believe you."

CHAPTER FIFTEEN

Levi's mom did not believe it. She and Levi were in the kitchen, a container of lukewarm stir-fry on the table as Levi tried, once again, through a mouthful of rice, to explain how he was entering a big tournament in Richmond free of charge.

"But you just started karate," his mom said, her voice dripping with skepticism.

Levi shifted. He knew where this was headed, down a long road about money and bills. "I know. It's hard to explain. But Mr. Anderson thinks I can do it. He wants to work with me."

Again, he wasn't sure how to put it into words. How Mr. Anderson expected so much from him. The way he spoke to him, worked with him. How his infectious energy made Levi believe he could actually win the tournament. Now Levi only wanted his mother to believe it too.

"Well, okay. But I don't want you to get hurt."

Levi smiled. He knew he had her now. "That's why I have the pads," Levi said. Oh, and he had a new belt, a bright, cautionary yellow one, that he was still wearing.

His mom looked away, but she was smiling too. "It's nice to see you so interested in something."

Levi poked around his plate. His mom had that look in her eyes, the one that came just before she got all corny and sentimental. "Don't start, Mom."

"What?" She reached out and ran a hand through his hair the way she did sometimes, touching him just to touch him. "And you must be really good, if he wants you in this tournament."

Levi shrugged. He wanted to be as good as Mr. Anderson believed he was, so he'd work harder than anyone to get there.

Karate class went well that week, the sessions afterward—not so much. Mr. Anderson continued to spar with him, continued to push him. Less smiles, more clapping, more sit-ups. At Fight Night, Mr. Anderson had him in the ring with Diego for round after round. Levi never scored a point. He came home and fell into bed before dinner, still dressed in his gi.

Gina posted the video from the park, and Kick City shared it again. And again, it did well, as Gina worked her magic, making him look like a star.

Noah and Jeremiah took notice. "Oh, look. There's the karate kid."

They laughed, circling Gina and Levi as they filed off the bus. Annoying, but Levi had noticed more recently how they didn't pluck his ears or smack his neck. No pushing or shoving. The promos were working there, too. Levi's tormentors kept their distance.

Gina shot them a quick glance. "Don't you guys have classes to get to? Potty training, paste eating, shoe tying, that sort of thing?"

"Aww, how cute. His girlfriend is taking up for him," Jeremiah said.

Gina was about to say something smart again, but Levi spoke first. "Hey, why don't you two come by Kick City?"

They went quiet and exchanged glances. Even Gina looked surprised.

Jeremiah scoffed. "Sorry, we're not losers who wear pajamas and pretend to do karate."

"I disagree—with the first part," Gina said with a smirk.

As they retreated, Gina smiled at Levi. "Look at you, standing up for yourself."

"I was recruiting."

Gina scrunched up her nose, watching the two boys go after their next target. "They aren't worth recruiting. Definitely not Kick City material."

That evening at class, Levi was distracted. He went through the motions during Circle Forms and struggled to get it right. His body was sore, and the upcoming tournament hung over him. How was he supposed to compete in less than two months? What was Mr. Anderson thinking? And when he wasn't worrying about the tournament, he had one eye on the window in case his dad decided to show up again, or even worse, showed up at the apartment.

Everything was cluttering up his mind when Mr. Anderson called his name.

"Levi, what are you doing?"

Levi stopped. Suddenly, all eyes were on him. "Huh? Nothing."

"Nothing, sir," Mr. Anderson corrected.

"Nothing, sir."

Mr. Anderson stared at him for a moment, then turned away. "I need you to stay with me here."

"Yes, sir."

Levi got through the drills and class ended. Then it was time for his one-on-one, a time he'd come to dread.

"You're not focused," Mr. Anderson said.

"I know. I'm sorry, sir."

And Levi meant it. His greatest fear was that Mr. Anderson would pull the plug on his free lessons. Would tell him he couldn't come to karate anymore.

His thirty-day pass was set to expire in a few days. Levi watched the calendar, knowing Mr. Anderson could take it all away whenever he wanted.

Levi was lost in the thought when Mr. Tabb approached and set his arm around his shoulders. "He was just thinking about the tournament, right, Levi?"

"Yes, sir," Levi said.

Mr. Tabb shot him a wink.

Mr. Anderson was not smiling; he was fixing the gloves on his fists. "Well, thinking about the tournament is great. Daydreaming, not so much." The gloves tight, he set on his head gear and motioned for Levi to do the same. "Let's go, get on your feet and start bouncing."

Levi bounced. They practiced blitzing techniques. Defensive maneuvers. He threw kicks and did leg locks. Mr. Anderson sparred against him, and while a few days ago Levi had been timid, leery to throw a kick or punch at his instructor, all that was forgotten after a week of grueling ninety-minute sessions.

Mr. Anderson came out of nowhere and punched him in the head. From there, Levi went to work. He fought to stay in the ring and in the fight. Mr. Tabb and the other black belts in the studio openly cheered for Levi.

Levi was drenched when Mr. Anderson landed a side kick to his midsection. He fell back just as his mother walked inside. She gasped, clutching her purse. Levi caught his breath and waved to his mom to let her know he was okay. She didn't look convinced. Her face was tight, jaw set. In her all-black waitressing clothes, she almost looked like a ninja ready to spar with the instructor.

"Okay, good work today, Levi," Mr. Anderson said, tapping his head.

Levi hobbled off the mat where he plopped down against the wall. His mother asked if he was okay. Levi assured her he was fine.

Mr. Anderson, still heaving from the match, did his best to calm her down. "It's all part of the sport."

She straightened and looked Mr. Anderson directly in the eyes. "I don't like violence," she said flatly, before she knelt to help Levi.

Levi caught Mr. Anderson's glance at the brace on her wrist before his gaze fell to the floor. Levi wasn't sure what was happening. Usually, Mr. Anderson was great with parents and knew just what to say. But now, his instructor seemed lost for words. So Levi got to his feet, set a big smile on his face, and told his mother all about how much fun he'd been having.

CHAPTER SIXTEEN

Mr. Anderson reminded himself to tread carefully. Although, Levi's mother seemed to be doing better now that Levi was on his feet, chugging down water and putting on a show about how much fun he was having. Mr. Anderson realized the kid was trying to put his mother at ease, and it worked.

"We're just going over some techniques. Levi here is a quick study."

Miss Rocco's eyes surveyed the room. She had a nice smile, even though she was obviously exhausted. She wore black clothes, like that of a waitress, and smelled a bit like food. But she was proud of her son. He could tell by the way she smiled at Levi, the pride brimming through her worried eyes.

"Thank you so much," she said. "For the classes and," she gestured around the room, "everything. I don't think I've ever seen him this happy." Again, she leaned in toward her son. "Are you sure you're okay? You looked hurt."

"Mom, I'm fine."

"Glad to do it," Mr. Anderson said. "He's really picking it up. I assume Levi told you the big news, about the upcoming tournament? It's in Richmond, June 26th, and I'd like for him to compete."

Her smile evaporated. Mr. Anderson already knew what was coming and didn't want to make this proud lady feel any more uncomfortable than she already did. "It's free of charge. I think Levi has a good shot at this."

Again, Mr. Anderson was cautious. He'd made a promise to Levi, to himself, to his wife, and even to Kenneth Keaton that this kid would win. But it was harder now, perhaps hardest of all, to tell Levi's mother what he'd done. And he couldn't get past the hint of skepticism lurking in her eyes.

Mr. Anderson nodded toward the back. "Can we talk? Just the two of us, in the back?"

Another flash of suspicion before Levi's mother nodded. She followed Mr. Anderson to the back as he removed the gloves and dabbed his forehead with a towel, still sweating from the sparring.

Once they were in the office, he gestured to a seat for Levi's mother. "A few things I wanted to say in private. First of all, tuition has been waived. I'd like Levi here full-time, as a student and a fighter."

The woman winced at the word fighter. She looked around the cramped office. "Mr. Anderson. I can't thank you enough for everything. I will say though, I'm a little apprehensive about the fighting, as you call it."

Mr. Anderson nodded. He'd been here before, mostly with mothers. Funny how the most gung-ho dads usually had the worst fighters. It was always the concerned mothers whose sons had the hearts of champions. "Completely understandable. But I want you to know you can trust me with Levi. I have his best interests at heart. I see a lot of my younger self in him, if I'm being honest." Where had that come from?

The woman's eyes snapped up, and she looked him full on

for the first time. Her gaze went glossy with tears before she looked away. "Is that your little boy?" she asked, nodding at the framed picture of Mr. Anderson's baby boy.

Mr. Anderson turned to the picture. "Sure is. That's Cody, Jr."

"He looks like you. Are you going to let him take karate?"

Mr. Anderson nodded. "Yes. I'll train him myself. If that's what he wants, of course."

Levi's mother closed her eyes as she smiled. "I hear you met Levi's father."

Mr. Anderson grimaced. "I did."

She studied him for a moment. "I don't know what Levi's told you about his father—if anything. But it hasn't been easy for him."

Mr. Anderson bowed his head. "I understand," he said quietly. And he did. He'd been through it himself.

Miss Rocco studied him closely, as though affirming something in her head. Then she shifted in her seat, straightening her back as though issuing a challenge. "I'm just going to be blunt with you. You can't let him down. He thinks so highly of you. I see it every day. And he gives himself so completely, that... So if this is something you're going to, I mean, if you decide–" She dug in her purse and found a tissue. "You can't let him down, okay?" The tears slid down her cheeks.

Mr. Anderson blinked away the sting in his own eyes under the weight of what she'd said. He cleared his throat. It was different this time, different from any other time with a parent. He leaned forward. "You have my word, Miss Rocco."

She dabbed her eyes. "Okay."

"With your permission, I will do everything I can to get Levi where he needs to be. He's got the raw potential to be the best fighter I've ever coached—I'm being completely honest with you. But I won't lie and say sparring isn't without danger. He wears the pads, but hitting and kicking is part of it."

She shifted in her seat.

Mr. Anderson did his best to put her at ease. "Again, he's safe here, with me. I'll protect him. I just want to be up front with you."

"I appreciate that," she said, taking a shaky breath. "Jeez, why couldn't he have gotten into soccer or theater? Maybe drawing."

Mr. Anderson laughed. "I think you know why. Your son is a fighter."

Back in the studio, Levi and his mother gathered their things and walked out, Levi still hobbling some but talking a mile a minute to his mother and trying not to show it as they got into the car and drove off.

Mr. Tabb stood beside Mr. Anderson. "Look, I know you bet the house on the kid, but you've got to ease up on him."

Mr. Anderson looked at him.

He shrugged and said, "He's good. I think he's got a chance to do well, but if you run him into the ground, he'll never have that shot."

Mr. Anderson sighed. "You're right."

Mr. Tabb stopped. He cocked his head. "I'm sorry, what was that?"

"You heard me."

"Can I get that in writing? Cody Anderson said 'you're right' and, what's today's date?"

Mr. Anderson punched him playfully. "Stop it."

No appointments the rest of the day. The two instructors started toward the office. It was time for the non-fun part—the recruiting, the books, the numbers.

"The kid's video is helping though. The park one. Had four

newbies talking about it as they walked in," Mr. Tabb said, picking a pad off the mat.

"Right? I tried to tell Kenneth that, that the videos would basically pay his way."

"Try not to tell Kenneth anything until after it happens. Remember that app he wanted? When he wanted to charge kids per class?"

"All too well. Now Pine Bluff is expanding. And we're here, in the empty lot."

"Yeah, but we could use this lot to our advantage."

"Hmm, you might be onto something." He looked back to the windows. All that empty space.

"That's what I'm saying. Oh, and look, again. I'm sorry I doubted you about Levi. He's a good kid, heck of a fighter too."

"Yeah? Maybe I'll write *that* down." Mr. Anderson clapped Mr. Tabb on the back. "But it's true, I've been losing focus. I just want to make this work. I want to expand Kick City, too, but I don't want to change how we do things. Does that make sense?"

"Absolutely. Hey, maybe we could reach out to Mrs. Keaton, maybe get some kind of scholarship thing going. She's into that sort of thing."

Mr. Anderson turned his gaze back to the empty lot before them. "Man, you're full of good ideas today."

CHAPTER SEVENTEEN

Levi had no idea why Mr. Anderson had brought him to the vacant parking lot at six in the morning on a school day. The sun was only dropping hints about rising over the studio, casting a grayish light over them that made Mr. Anderson seem like a ghost. A very direct, to the point ghost.

"Do you know why you're here?"

Levi wiped the sleep from his eyes. "I thought for karate lessons, but..."

Mr. Anderson almost smiled but cut it short. He paced a few steps, his hands clasped behind his back. "Sparring involves discipline. Skills, speed, strength, yes, but mostly discipline. And endurance."

It made sense to Levi. "Yes, sir."

"Here's how we're going to start. We'll run to the end of the lot. See down there, where the billboard is?"

Levi squinted. It looked about a football field away. "Yeah. Yes, sir."

"Then make your way up to the street, come around, and circle back to the store front. Five times."

Levi sucked in a breath. Five times around that loop had to be a few miles, easy. "Yes, sir."

"You sure about that? Didn't sound too sure."

"Yes, sir!"

Levi started off in a chuff, Mr. Anderson calling after him, "Got kids in that tournament who've been sparring for years, some of them most of their lives. Lot of ground to cover. But if you can't keep your breath, it won't mean anything."

Mr. Anderson's voice was still near, and Levi found Mr. Anderson was trailing him. "All those pretty kicks of yours, can't throw them if you're hunched over, out of breath. Pick it up."

Levi picked up his pace, his old shoes slapping the faded asphalt, kicking loose rocks over cracked pavement. His lungs were burning well before he reached the billboard, a sharp pain in his side as he came back around to the old Kmart.

Mr. Anderson seemed fine with the running, judging by the way he was talking. "You have to want it. Want it more than anything. Sure, it takes skill, endurance, and sometimes luck, too. But heart is what matters most. You've got the heart, Levi. We just need to bring it all together."

Levi was huffing too hard to respond. By the time he reached the billboard again, the second time, he wasn't so sure about the heart, definitely not the endurance. The urge to quit running screamed from inside him, daring him to go home and crawl back in bed. But Levi didn't quit, not with his instructor behind him, pushing him to keep going.

"Also," Mr. Anderson continued, hardly out of breath. "Defense. I want to train you to be a defensive fighter. Even if you have the kicks and the flash, we need to focus on blocking, reaction time. On your head movement," he said, bobbing his head around. "And of course, your footwork. If we can get those three down, we'll be getting somewhere."

Somewhere? They were circling a giant parking lot. Didn't

seem like they were getting anywhere. But Levi kept chugging forward. Another lap. He knew when he was being tested, and this sure felt like a test.

On the last lap around, it was all Levi could do not to fall on his face. They came to a stop at the truck, and Levi hunched over, hands on his knees. By then even Mr. Anderson seemed winded, although his looked to be a good type of winded, not a painful one.

"Take a moment. Then we'll get started."

Levi wiped his face on the sleeve of his shirt. Once he caught his breath, Mr. Anderson had him stretching.

"Okay, right side guard. Let's see it."

Levi broke into his stance.

Mr. Anderson turned. "Now, see the lines on the parking lot? When I say move, I want you to leap back. Then step and drag. Like this." Mr. Anderson set his guard and got into position. "But I never want you to cross the line. Got it?"

"But I can't see it."

"I want you to feel it," he said. "Like this."

They did the drag step, then the other guard. Mr. Anderson had Levi lean back, kick, then drag. Drag. Kick. Punch. Then again.

"Okay, nice work. That brings us to defense. Defense is crucial. And more importantly, defense is more than just blocking." He handed Levi a pair of gloves. "Now. I want you to punch me in the face."

Levi cocked his head. "What?"

"I won't punch back." He crouched into a stance. He had no head gear on as he stood in the lot, out in the open.

"You want me to punch you? In the face?"

Mr. Anderson flashed him a grin. "If you can. I'm going to show you how to defend yourself without blocking."

When Levi hesitated, Mr. Anderson gestured for him to bring it. "Come on, let's see what you got. Punch me."

For the next ten minutes Levi swung, heaved, and tried his best to punch his instructor's head. A few times he got close, but every time he had a clean shot, Mr. Anderson dodged it at the last second and Levi whiffed. Mr. Anderson, still with a smile on his face, would rear his head back, duck, or sidestep the punch just when Levi thought he had him.

He was impossible to hit, and it wasn't long before Levi was hunched over again, sucking down breaths.

Mr. Anderson patted him on the back. "It's all about footwork, Levi. You ready to learn?"

Levi nodded.

They went over footwork drills and defensive techniques until they lost track of time. Until the sun was up and bright and Mr. Tabb pulled into the lot. Only then, as Levi shuffled his feet, worked on side stepping, did Mr. Anderson seem to realize the time, and Levi remembered he had to go to school.

Mr. Anderson offered to give him a lift, but Levi wanted to ride the bus with Gina. He made it to the bus stop, barely, only to find Gina waiting, her hand on her hip and a smirk on her face.

"You okay?"

"Yeah," he said between pants. "Actually, no." His arms were wet, heavy ropes and his legs weren't much better off. "Been training."

Gina looked him up and down with a squint. "Really? Wow, you're taking this karate stuff seriously."

Levi plopped down on the grass, unconcerned with dirt or mud or anything else. He told her about the tournament.

"But you just started," she said with a smirk.

"Everyone keeps saying that."

"It's true. I mean, you're doing amazing, but *tournaments* already?"

"Yeah. Mr. Anderson thinks I can win."

Gina's smirk fell. "Win?"

"Yeah," he said, a bit irritable. He was tired, and was it really that impossible to believe he could win? Apparently so.

"Wow, that's, like win the whole tournament? Because I did some research when I was looking up the Kick City socials, and this invitational tournament is a really big deal, like all kinds of fighters."

"Maybe I should just quit, then. Is that what you're saying?"

Gina was hardly ever short for words, but now she only stood there, staring at him like he was an alien creature. Or worse, Jeremiah. "Okay, one—chill out."

Levi tried to chill out. "Sorry. Look, I know it sounds crazy. I'm not sure what Mr. Anderson is thinking. But he wants me to do it, so..." He picked at a piece of grass.

Gina's shoulders relaxed and she brushed her hair from her face.

Only then did he notice the streaks of pink in the blue. "I like your hair, by the way."

She opened her mouth like she was going to say something when the bus grumbled up the road. Gina fixed her bookbag, and Levi got to his feet, and then they were climbing aboard, taking their seats, and Levi kept wanting her to pop up and start talking, say something wild like she usually did. But she didn't.

It wasn't even eight and the day was a bust.

CHAPTER EIGHTEEN

All weekend, Mr. Anderson had been looking forward to Fight Night. Training was great. The kid was making remarkable progress, but now he wanted to see if the kid had made any real gains, which meant placing him head-to-head with Diego Martinez again. He needed to see how the kid would respond to the challenge. Also, he'd spent the better part of the afternoon talking with Mr. Keaton again (twice in a week), and he was itching to punch something.

He breathed a sigh of relief as Levi entered with a bow, his mother's Toyota pulling off in the lot. Mr. Anderson smiled. Some kids would have taken a week off after the workout the other morning.

Tony came to life just as soon as Levi sat down to stretch. "There's our superstar."

Mr. Anderson knew it was coming. Boosting Levi to yellow belt caused some jealousy, and now that the kid was going to fight in the tournament, egos were bruised, and scores needed settling. Mr. Anderson almost called Tony out but instead decided it would get worked out in the ring.

Emma plopped down beside Levi to stretch. Ten fighters

tonight. Most would enter the tournament in June, but it looked like only Diego and Levi, possibly Tony, had any real hopes to advance.

He lined them up and drilled them for ten minutes, then ten more. He had them practice blitzing with a partner, nudging Levi away from Emma to Tony, to go continuously for a minute, then two, until chests were heaving and brows were sweaty.

"All right," he said, setting up the ring. He relished this part, how the studio transformed from a nice family training center by day to survival of the fittest by night. And while Mr. Anderson loved everything about karate—from the forms students, the weaponry, to the basics, and the skills—it was the grit and heart of sparring that really got his blood flowing and his senses buzzing.

He wasted no time placing Tony in the ring. From there, he let anyone jump in who wanted a shot. Carlos, a blue belt, leaped in first and was quickly beaten 3-0. Emma forced herself forward next. Emma wasn't a natural fighter, but she was tough and worked tirelessly and kept coming back week after week. Mr. Anderson respected that about her.

Tony danced and taunted, his gloves dangling at his waist. Mr. Anderson would tolerate it for now, but as they got closer to the tournament, he would have to tighten up.

With Tony being sloppy, Emma managed to score a point. From there, Tony went to work. 3-1.

And then Levi jumped in.

The murmurs in the room fell to a hush. Levi fixed his helmet while Tony simply glared at him. The two fighters touched gloves and faced each other.

At the word *fight*, Tony attacked like a wild animal. The kid reacted like a pro and dodged Tony like he'd been doing it all his life. He followed with a quick punch to the head.

Point.

The parking lot lesson had paid off. Mr. Anderson marveled at the kid's poise, how calmly he reacted. Meanwhile, Tony shook his head, grumbling. He'd always been a hot head, but he was talented, nonetheless.

"Breathe, Tony. Clean technique, got it?" Mr. Anderson said as they lined up again.

This time, Tony backed off, and the kid circled the ring. Tony threw a few fakes, but Levi stayed put. It wasn't until Tony was in range, that Levi set him up with a skip kick to the ribs. When Tony blocked the skip kick, the kid countered with a swift hook kick to Tony's jaw.

Again, Tony started huffing, smacking his helmet with his hands. Mr. Anderson motioned for them to take their places, but Tony was already beaten, out of his head and angry. At *fight*, Levi blitzed, and it was over in an instant.

Tony ripped off his helmet and refused to tap Levi's glove.

"Tony, touch gloves," Mr. Anderson ordered.

Tony's face was red. His hair clung to his forehead. His eyes flashed. "Why?"

"Excuse me?"

"Why?" he screamed out.

Mr. Anderson turned to Diego. "Hold class." Then, to Tony. "You, in the back. Now."

Diego had Carlos line up to face Levi. Mr. Anderson stepped to the back and sat Tony down, not in the office but in the small storage room near the loading door. Chairs were set up for when he or Mr. Tabb brought prospective parents in for privacy to close the deal, something he hadn't been doing lately.

Tony fell into the seat, huffing and staring at the wall. Mr. Anderson took a chair and sat a foot across from him. "What's going on with the attitude? You're about to go for your junior black belt in a month, and you're out there acting like that?"

Tony stared past him, his chest rising and falling. Mr. Anderson could almost see the steam rising from his head.

"So that's it? Just going to throw it all away?"

"Why does it matter?" Tony snapped. "He's your favorite. All you care about anyway."

Mr. Anderson had figured there would be some jealousy. It came with the job. But he wasn't expecting so much anger. Tony glared at him, waiting for a response.

"So that's what this is all about? Levi?"

"You bumped him up a belt. You teach class for him. Then you coach him after class. Now he's in the tournament? I mean, what are we supposed to think?"

"You are supposed to worry about yourself. You are supposed to be prepared."

Tony exhaled loudly, again glaring at the wall. "I've been coming to sparring for a year, working my butt off, and now this new kid comes along, and you treat him like he's better than all of us."

Mr. Anderson straightened. "That's not what I'm doing. I'm giving him a shot because he's earned it. If you don't like it, beat him. Isn't that how Fight Night has always worked?"

Another huff from Tony.

Mr. Anderson leaned in. "You know what you have to work on. I've told you from day one."

"My temper."

"Your temper." He smiled at the kid.

Tony's face relaxed.

"Maybe if you didn't bull rush him every time, he wouldn't see it coming."

Tony shrugged. A small smile conceded the point. "Maybe."

"Yeah, maybe." He slapped his knee as he rose from the chair. "And you're welcome to a private lesson anytime you want one, got it?"

Tony closed his eyes, then nodded. "I'd like that."

"Done. Now come on, get out there. I'll give you another shot."

When they walked out, no one was sparring. Diego stood helplessly as the class stared at the door. Levi was nowhere to be found.

Mr. Anderson threw his hands up. "What's going on?"

Diego motioned to the door. "Some man came up, banging on the window. Levi said he had to go, and he took off."

CHAPTER NINETEEN

Levi had to get his dad away from the studio. Everyone in the room had turned to him as his father banged on the windows and demanded he come out. Levi's chest had tightened, and a shiver rode down his spine. It was just easier to go.

Now, in the truck, speeding down the road, he was doing his best to keep himself together, unsure he'd made the right decision. When his dad got like this, with that sharp gleam in his eyes, nothing good ever happened.

Levi had left his gear back at the studio. But there was no time to dwell on that, not as his father cursed, turning to him as they ran a red light and barreled down Crawford Avenue. "I'm going to let it slide how you were talking to me the other day, in front of that man."

When Levi didn't reply, it only prompted his father to keep talking. "Not sure who he thinks he is, either, coming out there talking to me like that. I'll kick his tail from here to Roanoke."

His mouth clamped shut, Levi glanced at his father, who took offense.

"What? You don't think I could? Just because he rolls

around on a mat all day like some pansy gymnast? Probably never had to work a day in his life."

Something must have shown on Levi's face because his dad shook his head. "Got something to say?"

Levi swallowed. He wiped his palms on his pants. "Where are we going?"

His father's jaw clenched. "See, why do you talk to me like that? I'm your old man, and I deserve some respect."

Respect was one thing he would never get from Levi. Too many late nights at the Med Center for that. And if he wasn't causing trouble for Levi's mother, he was plain gone. Disappearing for weeks, months, sometimes longer.

"Anyhow, thought we'd go out to eat," his father said.

"I'm not hungry."

In a blink, his father's hand slammed down on the steering wheel. Levi jumped as the truck skidded to a stop at a deserted gas station. His father moved to cuff him on the back of the head, but Levi dodged instinctively.

His father's eyes flashed with rage. "Dammit, boy, I'm not going to tell you again. You're going to start showing me some respect."

Again with the respect. Where was the respect for his mother? Or for him? He was only trying to take a karate class, and his dad kept busting in and making a mess of things. He'd been so jacked up for Fight Night, ready to prove himself for the tournament. But now, in that truck, with the stink of oil and tobacco in the cab, it seemed impossible that he could do such things. Levi peeked over to find his father glaring at him, his chest rising and falling angrily. Levi's gaze fell to his lap, and he mumbled an apology, wishing he'd just let his dad hit him.

Anything to get moving again. To get this over with.

They drove to Denny's, where Levi sat across from his father, pushing fries through ketchup, his hair matted and sweaty as they slogged through the world's most depressing dinner.

Levi's father nodded to his plate. "You just going to sit there and pout?"

Levi turned away from the window. "No."

"This karate stuff. What kinds of things they teaching you in there? How to fight, like, defend yourself?"

Levi managed a glance at his father. His beard was longer than last time, and there were more wrinkles around his eyes. Probably from jail. He'd been in and out of jail for the past five years, and each time it forged him into a meaner person. It made him hate the world just a little bit more every time he got out.

"Yeah. Tonight was sparring night." Levi couldn't bring himself to say "Fight Night" in front of his dad.

"Sparring?" His dad grinned in a way that was one part teasing and one part proud. "You kicking some tail in there?"

"I like it."

His dad picked up his double cheeseburger and took a big bite, talking through his mouthful. "Love to know how your mama is paying for that. I'm sure she'll be after me for money here soon."

Maybe for medical bills, Levi wanted to say, but he held back. And still, it was like his father heard the thought in his head.

"Got something you want to say?"

Levi shifted. Even in the restaurant, with the older men laughing about something in the back booth, Levi couldn't shake the grip of fear. He cleared his throat, but his voice was small and meek. "Well, karate is free."

"Free." His father snorted. "Boy, if there's one thing I've learned in this world, it's that ain't nothing free."

"It is. Mr. Anderson is letting me take classes for free."

"Why?"

"Just nice, I guess."

Another snort. His Dad ripped into his burger again, breathing through his nose as he chewed his food. Sitting at that booth with the taped and patched vinyl seats, Levi made a silent vow to himself to never, ever become like his father—a crusher of hopes and dreams.

His father took a slug of Pepsi, then wiped his mouth and pointed across the table. "Let me tell you something. He's got some motive, doing this. Those karate classes ain't free. I know that much."

Maybe it was because he needed something, a lifeline, something to pull him away from the stormy sea of his dad's eyes —eyes that were weighing him down, drowning him—but he sat up straighter. "I'm fighting in a tournament. That's why I'm training. Mr. Anderson said—"

"You know, I'm tired of hearing about this Mr. Anderson character. I took you out here so we could spend some time together. Father and son and all that. Not to hear about some man playing footsie with a bunch of kids."

Levi turned back to the window, watching a scatter of napkins dance in the wake of traffic.

His dad asked for the check. Once the waitress was gone, his father leaned over the table. Levi caught a strong whiff of onions. "People ain't just nice for no reason."

At twelve, Levi didn't know much about the world, but he hoped with all he had that his father was mistaken about that. And if he wasn't, Levi made another silent vow: he would prove his father wrong about people and motives—even if he had to do it himself.

CHAPTER TWENTY

As they pulled into the apartment complex, Levi tucked his hands under his legs and tried to keep his breaths low and even. They parked next to his mother's car, and Levi knew, whatever happened, he would not let his dad walk into that apartment. If he did, the yelling would start, which sometimes led to worse things. Things that brought them to the Med First Center.

To his relief, his dad didn't seem interested in talking to his mother. He sat back in his seat and looked over at Levi. "Was thinking maybe once I get settled, you could come stay with me sometimes."

It took everything Levi possessed not to turn and run. The last thing in the world he wanted to do was stay with his dad anywhere.

"Maybe," he managed, his gaze drifting to the apartment window.

"Maybe?" his dad scoffed. "I swear, you got some mouth. Well, tell you what. Once I find some work, I'm not forking over my entire paycheck to your mama for child support. You can tell her that right now."

The wind sucked out of Levi. His father's words from the restaurant came rushing back to him. *Nothing is free.* So that was why his father suddenly wanted to spend time with him—money. The trembling stopped. He set his hand on the door handle, feeling foolish for even thinking for a minute his father was trying to make things right. It was something, how his father could gut him so easily, even when he had his guard up.

When Levi didn't say anything, his dad put the truck back in gear. "Okay. I'll talk to you soon. Here she comes too. Tell her what I said, about staying with me. Maybe a few days during the week. We can split it up evenly. We'll see."

Levi wasn't sure how it happened so quickly. His mother ripped open the door and yanked him out of the truck. "Levi." Her voice was torn and strained as she shouted across the seat at his father. "How dare you come take him without my permission!"

"He's my son. I'll take him anywhere I please."

"The hell you will."

Silhouettes in the windows. The neighbors looked to see what was going on. It was happening again. Levi's hands and feet turned to stone. He was powerless to do anything but watch his mother's face come apart as she screamed at his father, who was still grinning but with that sharp gleam in his eyes. The gleam that meant trouble was coming.

His father reached for the door handle, and Levi forced himself to move. He tugged at his mother's arm and somehow managed to steer her toward the sidewalk. "Mom. Please. Let's go inside."

He was going to hurt her again. Levi couldn't stop him. He could hardly do anything. He didn't even know he was crying until his mom looked down and her eyes softened. She wiped his cheek, and all the fight rushed out of her.

"Oh, Levi."

His father was still yelling about money and child support and how he had rights as Levi's mother hurried him up the stairs for the door. Levi only wanted it to stop. Only wanted his father to go back to jail or away where he couldn't come and destroy everything good that had ever happened to him.

"See? See how this ends up? Got that boy out here crying like a sissy. I'll be talking to you soon," his father said, setting the truck in gear. He peeled out without a goodbye.

Levi was still wiping his face when another truck came down the hill. The two trucks passed each other. One was old and loud, the other shinier and newer.

Seeing it was Mr. Anderson, Levi broke free from his mother and shuffled down the steps to the landing.

Mr. Anderson let the window down. "Everything okay?" he said, before his gaze settled on Levi's face. "Hey." He hopped out of the truck. "What happened?"

Levi turned his head away to hide his eyes as Mr. Anderson approached.

His mother spoke. "I'm sorry. I'm... It was something with his father," she said, setting her hand to her forehead as though she were taking her own temperature.

Mr. Anderson nodded. "Yeah. I was wondering what happened to you. Came out and you were gone."

Levi was unable to lift his gaze from the sidewalk. "I'm sorry," he mumbled.

"No need to apologize. I was just... Sorry, I wanted to make sure you were okay."

Mr. Anderson looked back where Levi's father had torn out of the lot. He took a breath and sighed. He started to say something but stopped and looked around again, like he wasn't sure what to do or say. Levi's mother thanked him again and promised Levi would be at class tomorrow, but Levi still couldn't force himself to face his instructor like this. Not tonight.

Thankfully, Mr. Anderson didn't stick around. Once Levi and his mother were inside, his mother started pacing. Levi knew that meant she was thinking about something.

"Maybe we should move," she said. "Somewhere else, where he can't find us."

Levi wasn't prepared for that. His mother kept pacing, kept talking. "And I'm getting a restraining order. I'm done. I'm done living like this. I know he's your father, but—"

"No, he isn't."

She stopped pacing. "What?"

A surge of emotions boiled over in Levi's chest. "He's not my father. I hardly know him. All he does is hurt us. I don't want to ever stay with him, either."

"Oh, you are not staying with him. Trust me." She crossed the room and knelt in front of him, the way she did when she wanted his full attention.

Levi launched into her for a hug. He breathed in the familiar smells. Of the restaurant. Of the perfume she wore. He'd promised to protect her, it was why he'd started karate in the first place. And when the time came, he'd failed. He'd frozen up completely. Then he'd all but ignored Mr. Anderson. He'd ruined everything. All he could do was curl up to his mom and bury his face in her side.

Some fighter he was.

CHAPTER TWENTY-ONE

The kid was obviously terrified of his father. But Mr. Anderson wasn't sure what he could do about it. He was a karate instructor, not a social worker. He wasn't going to put his face in someone else's business. Then again, that was exactly what he'd done.

Mr. Anderson replayed the scene in his head. He wasn't sure why he'd driven to Levi's house. He'd panicked when Levi left the studio so abruptly. It was all he could do to call the matches.

Sure, the tournament was coming. And it was important. He needed the kid to have a clear head going in. He needed the kid to train without distractions. But this was bigger than the tournament. Bigger than karate. Mr. Anderson had seen the danger in the father's eyes. The man was capable of hurting people. And that brace on Levi's mother's wrist proved he already had.

That night, as he crawled into bed with his wife, he was torn between letting it go or doing more. The truth was, Tony had been right. He *was* favoring Levi. And Kick City was more than one student. It was about every student. But this kid had shown up for a reason. Mr. Anderson wasn't about to let him down.

He got to the studio early the next morning. He did his normal regimen of two-hundred pushups and one-hundred sit ups before an hour of training. He worked his weapons, nunchucks, bo staff, katana, and sticks. He was covered in sweat when Kenneth Keaton walked in at five minutes before nine. A promising day gone to the wayside.

"What are you doing here?" Mr. Anderson asked.

Kenneth Keaton smiled. "Oh, I was in town, figured I'd come over and see what was happening in the Maple Ridge parts."

Mr. Anderson mopped his face with a towel, mumbling to himself as Kenneth went to the desk and flipped through the attendance cards. It drove him crazy, how Kenneth barged into the studio and took control, fumbling through files and numbers. As far as Mr. Anderson was concerned, Kenneth could have the numbers, but the studio was his domain. Kenneth Keaton had no place on the mat.

Kenneth whistled as he scanned a checklist. "Hmm, we're going to need to run some promos. I plan to stop in at the local station this afternoon and price some promotions, then I thought I'd get to meet this boy of yours."

Mr. Anderson did his best to keep his composure. He made a fist and clenched until his knuckles bulged. "You're going to be here all day?"

"I think so." He looked up at Mr. Anderson and smiled. "Is that okay with you?"

Master Keaton, Kenneth Keaton's father, was an eighth-degree black belt. He'd fought in a war, then competed in karate tournaments all over the world. He'd always pushed Mr. Anderson to go further, through black belt training, mentorship, on to running his own karate studio. But as Mr. Anderson was approaching his sixth-degree black belt, it was only the breathing exercises he'd learned through martial arts that kept him from picking this small man up by the neck and setting him out with the trash.

"Sure, it's fine," he said through gritted teeth.

"Great," Kenneth said, popping his head up and surveying the room. "Oh, and hey, I was thinking, we should move these bags to the other side of the floor. Shift the front desk so it's facing the door. Those shelves are looking a bit shabby, too. All this paper. We need to get this place in order. Did I tell you how Pine Bluff is going digital? Going to have monitors on the wall so we can Zoom the classes, oh, and— Hey, where are you going?"

Mr. Anderson bowed off the mat, tossed the towel in his bag, stepped outside, and started running. He needed a few laps around the parking lot. Then a few more.

When he returned, Mr. Tabb had arrived, and Kenneth had recruited him to help audit the books. They were sorting through the attendance cards, the signup sheets, and seminar totals. Diego was there, too, and Kenneth was blabbing to anyone who would listen about the sleek new Pine Bluff studio. In fact, it was all he talked about.

"It's state of the art, right in town center, so it will get foot traffic as well. And it's completely wired up, as we're going mostly online, something we should've done years ago. Now we're playing catch up. Soon, I dare say that half of our new students will be virtual. Might get some of those VR goggles."

Virtual karate lessons. The thought made Mr. Anderson groan. Teaching karate through a camera lens was torture. He craved the human interaction, the sound of feet on the mat. The *hi-ya!* in the room.

Mr. Anderson busied himself with errands for most of the day, stopping at home for lunch to spend time with his family. It worked, he was in a much better mood by the time he returned to the studio, where he found everything had been rearranged. The desks, the bags, even the seats were in the wrong place.

By the time afternoon classes began to trickle in, Mr. Anderson had all but forgotten the lessons. But he was determined to show Kenneth the power of human interaction.

CHAPTER TWENTY-TWO

Levi arrived at Kick City for class a half hour early. He bowed coming in, then set his bag on the floor before he noticed something was different. Actually, everything was different.

"Hey, Levi," Mr. Anderson started. "Sorry, we've been doing some rearranging."

"Oh," Levi said, as the back door opened and out came the man with the BMW.

Something about Mr. Anderson, the way his jaw tightened whenever he was around the smaller man, told Levi class was going to be tough. But for now, the small man was coming for him.

"Levi Rocco, right?"

"Yes, sir," Levi said, as the man reached out and offered a limp shake of the hand.

"Kenneth Keaton, owner of Kick City Karate. I've heard great things. Great things, indeed."

Levi glanced around. Diego was helping restock the shelves near the desk. He and Levi exchanged glances. Diego shot him a smirk.

"So you're the one that's going to win the tournament, huh?" Kenneth Keaton continued.

"Oh, well, I don't know about that, sir," Levi said. He wished Mr. Tabb or Mr. Anderson would come in and rescue him from this extreme awkwardness. Awkwardness made worse because Diego Martinez, the best fighter in town, and maybe the state, was making no effort to hide his eavesdropping.

"Don't be modest. Mr. Anderson assures me you have what it takes. In fact, he's got a lot riding on you. Need to get you in the books, though. Get you some patches for that gi as well. We're running a special this week."

Levi jumped as Mr. Anderson clapped his hands twice and called the class to attention. "All right, let's get you warmed up." Three more loud claps and Kenneth Keaton flinched before he recovered.

"I'll let you get to it," he said with a wink.

The students hit the mat to stretch out as the little man got on his way. He looked to be enjoying Mr. Anderson's obvious discomfort; clearly there was some bad blood between them. Mr. Anderson stonewalled the man with his eyes, and Levi thought the guy should be more careful.

It took a bit, but soon he was in his BMW and headed for the Crawford intersection.

Mr. Anderson rolled his neck and shoulders. "Okay, class, we've got a lot to cover today. I want you focused and ready to work." Though he didn't seem so focused himself. He kept eyeing the front desk, which was now near the front door. Everything was out of place, and it was definitely distracting the instructor.

"Okay, pushups. Let's go. Let's go. Let's go!"

Levi dropped down to the floor. He was on his tenth or eleventh pushup when Mr. Anderson marched over and dragged the front desk across the floor back to its original position. With a grunt, he turned and shoved the hundred-pound desk into place. Once that was moved, he went for the shelves.

"That's it, keep it up," he said, rearranging chairs. The entire class was watching by the time he got them in place. "Don't worry about me," he said, his voice straining as he hauled a full bookshelf across the room. "Let's go. Circle Three."

They went through Circle Three, then Four. After a few corrections, they went back to Three and into Four, then did Three once again. Everyone was sweating and heaving by the time Mr. Anderson had them cool down and stretch again.

After class, the studio was back to normal. Levi stayed back to train. Diego stuck around as well, looking like he had a score to settle.

"Diego," Mr. Anderson nodded. "You staying back to train?"

"If that's okay, sir."

"Well, this is a one-on-one session, but it wouldn't hurt. Okay by you, Levi?"

Levi wasn't about to say no. After all, it wasn't like he was paying for the lesson. But as Diego put on his gear, calm and composed, Levi's stomach sunk at the thought of facing him.

"Okay, boys, on the line."

Mr. Anderson had them go through blitzing combos, then blocking combos. Mr. Anderson fixed Levi's footwork then had him blitzing again. Once they were sweating, Mr. Anderson said the words Levi had known were coming since he saw Diego hanging back after class.

"How about we have you two do some point sparring?"

Although they'd sparred before, things seemed more intense now. Besides, Diego had six or seven inches on Levi. He'd performed in local, regional, even national tournaments and was as quick as they came. And ever since that night Mr. Anderson called a questionable point for Levi, Diego had wasted no time knocking him around.

Mr. Anderson set up the cones. Mr. Tabb emerged from the back and took a seat on the row of chairs that had been returned to their place in the back. Kenneth Keaton had called Levi out in front of Diego, and now there was a vibe in the room. And it wasn't one Levi liked much. At least not at first.

With a quick glance outside as Levi set his helmet on his head, he thought about his father showing up, forcing him to a sad dinner at a sad diner where they sat across from each other. How his mother had fought with everything she had. The way her face changed, the deep power in her voice. It was clear she would die to protect Levi.

It was while Levi was thinking of his mother, her fighting spirit, that something happened to his body. It started with the thump of his heart in his ears. His lungs opened up, and his blood thrummed through his veins like oil inside an engine.

In the ring, the two fighters faced each other. They tapped gloves, and for all Levi's worries and troubles, he knew this was the one thing he could control in his life. He couldn't control his father or his mom working late all the time. He couldn't control the bullies on the bus or his dirty shoes or how he was invisible in the hallways at school. But here, on the mat in this room, he had all the control in the world over what was going to happen.

At the word *fight*, Diego blitzed. Levi sidestepped, dodging the backfist before snapping back, away from the follow-up blow. When Diego missed, Levi threw a kick to the fighter's mid-section and connected. Diego let out an "umph."

Mr. Anderson actually jumped. "Point!"

Levi caught Mr. Anderson glance over to Mr. Tabb before the instructor smiled at Diego. "Looks like you got some competition tonight, Mr. Martinez. Step it up, champ."

To his credit, Diego didn't throw his helmet or even show

any emotion after the initial surprise. He simply glanced down and nodded to himself. Then he lined up and started bouncing.

Levi was bouncing as well. He was lighter, stronger, ready to charge through the brick walls if needed. Mr. Anderson said, "Fight," and he sprang into action.

He still had his guard up, as Mr. Anderson had drilled defensive techniques into him. But he was no longer hanging back. He closed the gap between him and the long fighter before him. Distance was a problem with a fighter like Diego, whose kicks seemed to stretch across the room. With that in mind, Levi took the distance, sealing him off.

With his kick neutralized, Diego tried to back off, make some space, but Levi stayed on him, weaving as he'd learned in the parking lot and spent hours practicing in his room. When the gap came, he took the opening and struck quickly, a lightning fast shot to the ribs that nearly folded the taller fighter onto the mat.

"Point."

Mr. Tabb was on his feet as he edged closer, his eyes wide and unblinking. Only the sound of the fighters' steps on the mat filling the room. Diego composed himself, but through the protective shield on his helmet, Levi caught a flash of surprise on his face.

They lined up again. And Diego, a fighter who'd won a few tournaments, been regional champion, who'd hardly ever been challenged inside the walls of Kick City, now looked thoroughly shaken.

On the next clash, Levi once again closed and took the kick away. Diego threw a quick strike. Levi brushed it off with ease but managed to stay close, bobbing left to right, ducking, and becoming a moving target that couldn't be hit. When Diego did manage to back off, Levi faked a blitz, and that was all it took.

Diego leaped back and put up his guard. Levi skipped into a side kick to the ribs.

And then it was over, 3-0. Levi had beaten the regional champ. He looked around, then down at his gloves as though they weren't connected to his hands.

Mr. Anderson stood staring at him.

It was Mr. Tabb who spoke first. "I do believe we have a chance at that tournament."

Finally, Mr. Anderson nodded. "All right. Let's do it again. Come on, Diego, let's get our head in the game."

They sparred again. Diego won 3-1. Then again, and Levi won 3-2. They did one more, until Levi was so tired, he could hardly get his guard above his hips.

When they were done, Diego approached Levi. His face was flushed and sweaty, with red splotches on his cheeks. "Way to fight, man."

"Thanks."

"Don't thank me," he said, and Levi forced himself to look up. Diego's face was tight, serious, his brown eyes gleaming. "Keep working, got it? I won't give you anything and same for you with me. It's nice to have some competition in here and we're going to push each other to the championship. And then," he said, with a smile, "I'll get my revenge."

Levi nodded, smiling back at Diego. "Sounds like a plan."

CHAPTER TWENTY-THREE

"Did you see that?"

"Indeed, I did."

"You saw that, right?" Mr. Anderson paced the floor. "Did you see how he..." He ducked, weaved, and bobbed around then threw a backfist. "Caught him in the ribs like that?"

Mr. Tabb pointed to the floor with both index fingers. "I was right here."

"I mean, how he closed the distance so Diego couldn't kick. Come on. How smart was that?"

"Very smart, sir. Well trained too."

"Instinctive, skilled, and naturally talented. He's the perfect mix."

"Okay, okay. Again, I concede. I'm impressed. You saw it right off with the kid. I needed convincing. Consider me convinced."

"But," Mr. Anderson said, shoulders slumping, "there's always a *but* with you."

Mr. Tabb smiled, then he shrugged it off. "*But*. It's just that, well, you're still taking a huge risk with him. Do you expect him to fight like that every night, when the lights come on and the tournament comes around? It was only four of us here tonight. Wait until there's a panel of judges, a crowd. The real thing, that's all."

"I'm way ahead of you, sir."

"Of course you are, sir."

"We're going to do an in-house tournament."

Mr. Tabb nodded. "Ah, another one of those."

"No, not here, though. At the mall."

"The mall? Really? So that's what you did all day, schemed up a plan, huh? Hmm, that could be cool. I suppose Mr. Keaton would be all about the promotion."

Mr. Anderson scowled at the name.

"Sorry."

Mr. Anderson got back on topic. "Like a demonstration. We'll do Circle Forms, weapons training. Sparring."

"This could work. When?"

"Two weeks from this weekend. We need to get Levi out there, get his first tournament under his belt."

"Wait, so we're doing all this for the kid?"

"Don't start. Like you said, Kenneth will love it. But...let's tell him afterward. I don't want him coming down here and being a buzzkill."

Mr. Anderson had, in fact, been scheming. While he'd been out avoiding Mr. Keaton, he'd secured a four-hour window at the nearby shopping mall. It wasn't as hard as he'd thought it would be. The mall seemed itching to get people in there for events.

Now, with the plan in motion, he printed up posters, and spent the last ten minutes of every class that week reminding students to show up. Beginners, advanced students, he needed them all to come, any skill level was welcome. "This is your time to shine," he told the class, urging them to take part. "Tell your friends!"

He was feeling good about things. About recruiting. About getting the kid some experience. He phoned his old friend, Ms. Fleming, over at Pine Bluff and asked her about bringing some kids down for a small event. She accepted. It looked like Levi was going to do his first tournament.

Things were humming along. Three new students arrived, and all three signed up. Mr. Anderson buzzed around, brimming with energy, as Mr. Tabb led beginner class. They were all bright and crisp in their new creased gis, ready to learn. And he was ready to teach.

And then Kenneth Keaton struck again.

Mr. Anderson closed his eyes as Kenneth entered the studio. The guy was coming down almost weekly now, which was far, far too often. He sauntered in, and the class turned their heads. Kenneth never bowed when he entered, never bowed onto the mat. He had zero respect for the very thing Mr. Anderson stood for and strived to uphold.

Kenneth did a double take at the furniture, now back in its original position. At least Mr. Anderson got some satisfaction there, short lived as it was.

Mr. Anderson had retreated to his office.

Kenneth opened the door. "What's this about a mall tournament?"

So much for keeping things a secret. "Hi, Kenneth. Good to see you."

Kenneth waved away the pleasantries as he took a seat. "Were you planning on telling me about this? I had to hear it from Fleming."

"You drove all this way to ask me that?"

"I drove down to check in with my underperforming store."

"School. Dojo. Studio. Not a store."

"Oh, spare me. At the end of the day, we're here to turn a profit."

Mr. Anderson set down his pen and smiled, as though he were facing the villain in a spy movie. "Yes, and we *are* making a profit for you. But for some of us, mainly my students, this is a school. My students come first. They always will. Your dad would've said the same thing."

Kenneth balled up his face. "Don't drag my father into this."

"Your father is the reason we're here," he said, his voice rising.

Kenneth Keaton got to his feet. "Look, you may think you had some special bond with my dad. And maybe you did. But I'm running this now. Me. And as long as you're a part of the Kick City family, you will do things my way, got it?"

"Funny, because you just said it. *Family*. How can you go against everything your father stood for and then call it a family? And your mom, what does she think of all this bottom-line stuff?"

Kenneth turned away. "I'm not doing this with you again. And this mall tournament. Have you thought about insurance costs? Logistics?"

"Have you thought about the publicity? The signup sheets? The recruitments?"

Mr. Anderson smiled as the man's eyes went dreamy before he blinked. "Yes, of course, but it's still a risk."

"Everything is a risk, Kenneth. But you wanted us to expand and grow. You told me to get creative. That's what I'm doing."

"Well, I suppose."

It was a small victory, getting the best of his nemesis. Mr. Anderson got to his feet and clamped a hand on Kenneth Keaton's shoulder, causing him to wince.

"I've got a class to teach," he said, deciding he couldn't be in the room any longer. "Hey, want to join? Hit the mat for a bit?"

Kenneth's eyes bugged out of his head. He fixed his collar

and looked around. "Um, no. Actually, I'm just here to update some software, and then I'll be on my way."

"Okay, but if you change your mind..."

"I won't," Kenneth said, taking a seat at the desk.

Works every time. Mr. Anderson smiled. And then he walked out the door and to the mat, leaving everything he hated about karate for everything he loved.

"Who's ready to work?!"

CHAPTER TWENTY-FOUR

"So, you are going to do karate at the mall?" Gina struggled to see the allure of a mall tournament. That, and she just liked to mess with Levi.

"No, it's a tournament. I don't know all the details, just that people are going to be watching."

That was the part troubling him. It was one thing to spar in the safe confines of the studio, to try and fail and learn in the process, but the thought of a crowd gathering just to watch him fight made his breath a little shaky.

"Okay, okay. I can work with that. We can call it, *Mutiny at the Mall*," she said in a deep voice. "No, no, how about *Mayhem at the Mall*? Something like that? I can do some graphics for the promo. This might be kind of fun."

She was giggling, but Levi didn't see the humor. "I'll probably make a giant fool out of myself."

Gina looked up from her phone. "Don't do that, Levi. You're good. You have to know that. And even if you did make a fool out of yourself, it's just the Maple Ridge Mall. Nothing spectacular, no offense."

"I've only been sparring for a few weeks."

"Wait, hang on. When I said that, you got all pouty with me. Besides, I thought you said you beat Diego the other night?"

"Yeah, then he beat me. Twice. And maybe it was just a fluke."

"Doesn't sound like it."

The bus pulled up and they hopped aboard. As soon as they took their seats a balled-up piece of paper hit Levi in the back of the head. Jeremiah called them "the cutest reject couple."

Gina shot Levi a look. "Besides, wouldn't it be great to show those idiots what you can do?"

THAT NEXT WEEK, Mr. Anderson was all business. The familiar smile gave way to a razor-sharp focus on details and footwork. He called Levi out in class, usually for something he wasn't doing correctly or without enough intensity. The classes as a whole did more pushups, more leg holds, and a lot more stretching than ever before.

"We have a tournament coming up, folks. Again, I want everyone to be there. Sparring, forms, weapons. It's an integral part of martial arts to push yourself beyond your comfort zone. It's how we get better. How we grow."

So far, seven people had signed up for sparring, a list that included Diego, Emma, Tony, and Levi. And at least ten sparrers were coming down from Pine Bluff. It made Levi jittery.

Mr. Anderson noticed.

As they were going through Circle Three, Levi fell behind and never caught up.

"Levi, you okay over there?"

The entire class looked his way.

"Yes, sir."

Mr. Anderson tapped his temple with his fingertip. "Focus."

That night, Levi and his mother were at the laundromat when he finally broke the news about the mall tournament. She dropped the shirt she was folding. "Really? This weekend? And you're just now telling me?"

"It's just a small thing, not the big tournament."

She was already shaking her head. "This is not some small thing." Her excitement sputtered. "This is for the fighting?"

"Sparring. Yes."

She picked up the shirt, muttering how she wasn't so sure about all of this. Levi promised it would be fine and reminded her about the pads and eventually she must have believed him, judging by her smile. Casually, he asked if she'd heard anything else about his father.

The smile dropped like an anvil. "No, I have not. But I still mean to get over to the police station and file a report."

Levi knew it wouldn't happen. Be it pride or fear, his mother would never file any report or restraining order. She would only hope he wouldn't do it again. But he would do it again. He always did it again.

It was part of the reason Levi kept training so hard. It was why he'd taken to doing another round of sit-ups and pushups in his room before bed and when he got up in the morning. It wasn't showing yet, but his body was screaming from all the extra work. He even did his own leg holds, pushing against his wall and throwing the kicks as high as he could, slowly, until every muscle burned like it was on fire.

He'd come to love that burn, to feel as though something was happening, changing. Because if his young life had taught him anything, it was that change was good. Anything beat sticking around, like his mom did, waiting for someone else to strike.

Sure, it was great to be a defensive fighter, as Mr. Anderson had trained him, but he was ready to go on the offensive and force things to happen.

CHAPTER TWENTY-FIVE

The girl with the blue hair was talented. Mr. Anderson would give her that. A few days before the mall tournament, Gina had sent Kick City her latest promotional video. Mostly a mash up of Levi and his kicks, pulsing music in the background, along with wide shots of students in the studio punching and kicking in unison, before closing with a still of the Maple Ridge Mall.

And yeah, *Mayhem at the Mall* was a bit much, but she'd obviously spent a lot of time and effort making the video, and it had already amassed a few thousand views.

Now, as Mr. Anderson set up chairs in the empty shopping mall, he stopped and took a look around. It wasn't much, enough for a few mats, a ring, a floor for the performers. He wondered how Levi would perform in front of an audience.

The kid was holding his own with Diego on Fight Night. It seemed he could still find a way to wow Mr. Anderson every chance he got, but tournaments were a different beast. It was sink or swim for fighters, battling the pressure as well as the opponent. If Levi folded at this mall demo, he'd have his work cut out for him to be ready to go for the Invitational come June.

Mr. Anderson forced himself to let it go, to focus on the studio as a whole. He had sixteen kids competing today, and he was determined to coach all of them.

Ms. Fleming also had ten students coming down. He knew at least three of them were the real deal, experienced fighters near Diego's level. If Levi could compete here, win a few matches, Mr. Anderson would feel good about his chances going in. The shuffle of feet stole his attention.

"Are you doing that look around thing again?" Mr. Tabb said, approaching with two duffle bags.

Mr. Anderson laughed. "What look around thing?"

"You know, one of your famous hands-on-hips moments, where you soak it all in before the craziness starts." He nodded to Mr. Anderson's hips, where his hands had come to rest. "That."

Mr. Anderson dropped his hands. "We've done a lot of stunts over the years, but a mall tourney is a new twist, huh?"

Mr. Tabb dropped the bags. "It's new, that's for sure." He sniffed the air. "Man, the food court is already cooking?"

"Remember the middle school demo in the cafeteria?"

Mr. Tabb laughed. "You mean the stampede? Learned a lesson there, didn't we? No free candy. Those kids were on a sugar high and looking for a brawl."

"And there was that county fair a few summers back. You fought that donkey." Mr. Anderson said with a laugh.

Mr. Tabb rubbed his backside. "I did not fight that donkey. That donkey was out for blood."

The two men chuckled over old times as they hung the banners, taped off a space for the ring, for demos, then finished setting up folding chairs for the audience.

Mr. Tabb seemed to know what was on Mr. Anderson's mind. "You think he'll be okay?"

Mr. Anderson shrugged. "I guess we'll find out, won't we?"

"Guess we will."

The mall opened its doors at eleven, and it wasn't long before the place was getting foot traffic. The gates to the stores rolled up, and things were underway. Soon, Diego, Emma, and the rest of his team arrived. The demo was set for a one p.m. start. Ms. Fleming arrived with the Pine Bluff kids a little before noon. Mr. Anderson greeted everyone with his regular gusto of high fives and encouragement as they arrived. No sign of Levi yet.

Mr. Tabb was handing out thirty-day passes left and right. The chairs were filling up, and there was a good number of people standing around, waiting to see what was going to happen.

By one o'clock the kid was still a no show. Worse still, Kenneth Keaton had connected himself to Mr. Anderson's side, peppering him with questions about costs, recruits, and mall insurance policies. Mr. Anderson managed to escape long enough to call Levi's mom, but there was no answer.

When he returned, Ms. Fleming asked if he was ready to go.

Mr. Tabb, who'd set up a sound system, handed Mr. Anderson a mic. "Sorry, sir, but the show must go on."

Kenneth Keaton followed Mr. Anderson, who took the mic and nodded. "Showtime," he said to Kenneth as he put on his happy face and took the mat.

"Good afternoon, people of Maple Ridge! How are you out there?"

Where Mr. Anderson wasn't good at numbers, he was good with people. He had no fear of public speaking. Well, that wasn't entirely true. When he was younger, he stuttered and stammered and was terrified of everything. But karate had given him confidence, the courage to face whatever was crazy enough to set itself in front of him. Along the way he'd found he had a way with crowds. These days, no coffee could compete with the boost of adrenaline he got from karate tournaments. He relished the opportunity to show off his skills.

"We have a packed show for all of you. We'll have demo teams, dance, weapons, and of course, sparring. So stick around, and if you like what you see, or if you've ever dreamed of getting your black belt but keep finding excuses why you can't do it, today is your day to change all of that. Now, here with me is the son of Master Calvin Keaton, who started Kick City from scratch nearly thirty years ago. Let's all give a warm welcome, to Kenneth Keaton."

It was a dirty move, putting Kenneth on the spot like that. But Mr. Anderson couldn't help himself. Watching Kenneth blush and squirm gave him the satisfaction he needed to forget about the kid standing him up, at least for a bit.

"Well, um. Thank you for that, Mr. Anderson," Kenneth said through gritted teeth. "Yes, um, we're all here for a show." Then, coming to life, a gleam came over his eyes, and he warmed up and rambled off all the social media channels. A quick smirk toward Mr. Anderson, and he continued, "Oh, and don't forget, if you're out in Pine Bluff, we're breaking ground on a new location, it's going to be a great facility, and—"

Mr. Tabb cued up the music.

Mr. Anderson wrestled the mic from the owner. "Okay, time for some karate."

With that, the demo team took the mat. Emma nailed a routine she'd been working on for months, and Mr. Anderson cheered them on, still keeping an eye out for the kid. He had a terrible feeling something awful had happened, with his father or worse. But he couldn't just leave to go search the town for him. He'd set this up and this was it.

Kenneth Keaton sidled up beside Mr. Anderson. "Nice try,

putting me on the spot like that. And just so you know, Pine Bluff isn't your competition. We're a family."

"Family, huh? What a concept. Well, I can tell which child is the favorite."

"Ha ha. Get your numbers up and maybe you can get out of that crap hole you call a studio. Now, where's the kid?"

"He'll be here," Mr. Anderson said, hoping he sounded more confident than he felt.

Emma performed a solo form as the crowd—now filling chairs, some standing along the ropes—let out a gracious applause. Next was the weapons demonstration, and Diego led the way with four others to run through a bo staff exhibition.

"He's not coming, is he?" It was clear Kenneth Keaton was enjoying this. "You said this kid was good, and maybe he is, but little help that does you if he won't show up. This is what I'm talking about, Cody, you can't put all your eggs—hey, where are you going?"

Mr. Anderson knifed through the crowd, a smile peeling his face back as Levi came rushing to the scene, his shoelaces trailing his steps as he struggled to get his belt tied.

Mr. Anderson exhaled with a laugh. The kid hadn't even been taking karate lessons long enough to learn how to properly tie his belt, and yet Mr. Anderson had bet his career on how well he'd fight at the tournament.

"Sorry, sir. My mom's car broke down, and I had to wait for the bus."

Mr. Anderson noticed a grease stain on the sleeve of his gi. Guilt hit hard. "The bus? Why didn't you call me?"

"Phone died. Besides," the kid looked around, "with the tournament going on and all..."

"Still," Mr. Anderson started, dropping to a knee to fix the kid's belt, "next time call, okay? Is your mother okay?"

"Yeah, she's got a friend from work coming to look at the car later, so…"

Obviously, the kid was no stranger to setbacks. Mr. Anderson remembered those days as well. No money for back-to-school shopping, birthdays, vacations. Christmas. Being one break away from completely broke. But no time for all that now.

"Are you ready to fight?" he asked, looking into the kid's eyes.

Levi nodded. "I think so."

Mr. Anderson took him by his shoulders. The kid's eyes were swimming. "Look, we've discussed this. Some things are out of our control. Cars break down, parents fight, the weather turns cold. Rain happens. But right now, in here, it's all you. You have control now, Levi. You have what it takes to win this, you hear?"

The kid's chest rose and fell as he looked around before his eyes met Mr. Anderson's. "Yes, sir."

"Are you sure? Do you understand? Because you can do this. I know you can. I've been doing this a long time, and I'm telling you right now that you have what it takes. That doesn't mean you will win simply by walking on the mat. It's going to require everything you've got. You have to believe it. Do you believe it?"

Levi nodded. "Yes, sir. I do."

"That's it. Now, remember defense. Remember to blitz when I tell you to blitz. Don't second guess, just go. Got it? Listen to what I say and react. Are we clear?"

"Yeah," he said, then shook his head. "Yeah, sir."

Mr. Anderson clapped him on the back. "Go get stretched out. I'm putting you in after Emma's match."

"Who am I fighting?"

"Doesn't matter. It never matters who you are fighting. Get yourself prepped, and I'll handle the rest."

The kid went to stretch, and for the first time that day, Mr. Anderson took in the day's bright sunshine streaming in through the skylight. *Well okay*, he thought, *this just might turn out to be a good day*.

CHAPTER TWENTY-SIX

To Levi, it seemed like everyone in Maple Ridge had come out to the mall to watch him fight. He found a place to plop down and stretch amongst the bags and equipment. He was coiled tight and couldn't shake the chill that rattled him from the inside out. The air conditioning was pumping, and his arms were covered with bumps. His heart thumped and his feet were concrete. The hairs on his head were icicles. Nothing was right.

Levi cheered as Diego breezed through his first fight, 3-0 in under two minutes. The crowd gave a booming applause when Diego landed an impressive hook kick to his opponent's head for the victory.

Emma and Tony high-fived him as he came off the mat and removed his helmet. When Levi held his hand up, Diego took one look at him and quit smiling. He shook his head. "Follow me."

Levi did as he was told, wondering what he'd done to upset his teammate. As Emma took the floor to face a boy named Cole from Pine Bluff, Levi backtracked, following Diego behind a row of chairs reserved for the studio.

Diego ripped his padded gloves off. "You're scared."

It was a statement. Levi wasn't sure how to answer. Diego was right, Levi was beyond scared. He was terrified. All those people were watching, screaming and cheering. It was too cold. The lights too bright. The other fighters were too fast. In the distance, he heard the judge call, "Point."

Diego stuffed the gloves in his bag and rolled his neck. "It's normal. This is your first tournament and all. But you gotta fight through it, okay?"

Levi tried to swallow but his throat was closed off. He nodded. In a flash, Diego tapped him twice on the jaw. *Smack. Smack.*

Levi jerked his head back. "What are you doing?"

"I'm hitting you. The sooner you get hit, the sooner you can get over the nerves. Turn it on and fight, man."

Diego went to hit him again, and Levi dodged out of the way.

Diego smiled. "There it is."

Another point out on the floor. Emma had her head down and her shoulders slumped.

Diego shook his head. "Poor Em, I wish her parents would let her focus on demo instead of sparring."

"What do you mean?"

"She hates sparring. And I don't mean that as a put down. Em's awesome. She crushed it in demo. But sparring isn't her thing."

The match on the mat ended. Diego popped Levi in the head again. "All right, get yourself together. I think you're fighting that Drew kid. If I remember correctly, he's a defensive guy, so you'll need to make your move, otherwise the two of you will dance around the mat all afternoon."

Levi nodded. "Okay, but why are you helping me?"

Diego stood straight up, towering over Levi. He shot him a

sly grin, his brown eyes shining. "Oh, I'm not helping *you*, I'm helping me. I need you in the finals."

"You need me? Why?"

"Because I still owe you some payback, superstar. You think I forgot?"

The pep talk with Diego helped some. As did the pops to the head. But Levi was still tight, as though he'd been stuck in a cooler overnight and needed to thaw. As he stepped onto the mat for his first fight, he tried to loosen up, move around and get a feel for things. It helped that Mr. Anderson stood directly behind him, and to his surprise, Tony, Diego, and Emma were there as well, cheering him on.

Let's go, Levi!

You got this!

Drew, the kid he was facing, chewed on his mouthpiece as they met at the center of the mat. He didn't look too impressed, and for good reason. Levi was lost from the start. As soon as they touched gloves, Levi forgot everything he'd ever learned.

Someone yelled "Fight!"

Drew circled him like a cat, crouched low with one arm out in front, as though he were testing the waters before him. Levi tried to focus, but there was so much to see, so much noise. The people, the mall, the shoppers with phones aimed at him. Everything seemed to be swimming around them.

Mr. Anderson yelled at him. Diego was yelling. Everyone was shouting something different, and before Levi knew what to do with his hands, the other fighter had struck him in the face with a backfist, scoring the first point of the match.

Levi dropped his head in shame.

Mr. Anderson called him in and forced his chin up so their eyes could meet. "There, he scored. That's the worst that can happen." He shrugged, then leaned in with a devilish smile. "Now let it go and fight."

Staring at his instructor, the lightbulb popped on. Levi blinked in astonishment. Mr. Anderson was right. The other fighter had scored. It wasn't life ending or shattering. It was a point. Just a point. A boost of adrenaline jolted Levi ramrod straight before he shook his head, left to right, right to left. Then he got in position, right side guard. He started bouncing.

The ice thawed. The mat was no longer cold but squishy and soft, the same as in the studio. The padded gloves were once again an extension of his hands. He closed his eyes and remembered the day he beat Diego. The mall went silent. His body was fluid and nimble, like it belonged to him once again. He could do this.

At *fight*! Drew, the defensive fighter, smelled blood and rushed in for the kill. Levi, now bouncing with vigor, stepped back and landed three lightning-fast kicks to his ribs.

Mr. Anderson leaped a few feet into the air. "That's it, Levi!"

Levi smiled at the sight of his instructor and team getting so excited for him. The clash had lasted less than three seconds, and now the match was tied.

On the next round, Drew dropped back, his hand out and his senses back in place. He was a smart fighter and wasn't about to make the same mistake twice. But Levi was charged and revving now. This time, when Mr. Anderson told him to blitz, he did just that.

Levi shot in like a lightning strike, one arm up before he landed a backfist to his opponent's chest. Point. 2-1.

Levi turned and got into position, biting down on his own mouthpiece so everyone wouldn't see how hard he was cheesing. Now he was feeling it. His limbs were weapons, instruments he could wield in a number of different ways. He'd tuned out the distractions. The mall, the crowd, the bings and dings, all distant background noise. Levi only saw his opponent.

He bounced in anticipation, ready to go just as soon as the word was called.

The next round was over in a blink. Mr. Anderson said the word, and again Levi didn't fake, didn't hesitate. He simply pounced on the fighter and landed a skip side kick to the ribs. Match.

He won his first ever official sparring match 3-1, and by the time he stepped off the mat, the other fighters were crowding him, smacking his head and his back.

Tony won his match, and Kick City was holding their own with Pine Bluff. In fact, they went 5-3 in first-round head-to-head matches with their rival school.

Diego cruised through the second round, winking at Levi as he walked off the mat in victory. Mr. Anderson was still chatting with Kenneth Keaton, or rather, Kenneth Keaton was chatting while his instructor looked to be doing some sort of meditation exercises.

Emma lost her second match, and Levi sat beside her as she came off the mat.

"I suck," she said, her helmet in her lap.

"You really don't."

Emma ripped her gloves off in a huff. "Um, did you *see* that fight?"

Levi shrugged. "It's just one fight. I heard you crushed it in demo."

Emma cut a glance over her shoulder. "It was two fights, actually. I lost both. And tell my mom that."

"So, don't take this the wrong way, but do you like sparring?"

Emma stuffed her helmet in her bag. "No, not at all. But my mom makes me do it, she says I shouldn't give up on things."

"Even things you don't like?"

"Like I said, try telling her that."

"But you're really good at karate. I've seen you help the little kids with forms. Maybe you could be an instructor one day."

Emma's eyes brightened as a hint of a smile flashed across her face before it vanished with a sigh. "Well, I do like karate, and demo. Just not sparring. Does that make sense?"

Levi nodded.

Emma laughed. "No, not to you it doesn't. You love it."

"I don't *love* it," he said.

Emma laughed. "You totally do," she said, giggling harder now.

"I guess I don't hate it. But you obviously love demo. And I've seen you out there. I could never do that."

Emma's smile fell. "I just need a way to tell my mom."

Levi remembered how Diego had given him advice before he went in the ring with Drew. Maybe that was part of karate, too, supporting friends and teammates. "Well, I'd try being honest with her. Maybe after today, with two first place medals, your mom will see what you can do. And you should talk with Mr. Anderson about it."

Emma smiled, nudging him with her shoulder. "Wow, and here I thought you were just a meathead fighter."

Mr. Anderson appeared before them. "Levi, you're up."

"Okay," Levi said, getting to his feet. "Wish me luck."

"You don't need it, but good luck!" She looked over at the mat. "Oh, you're fighting Cole. Avenge me!" she called out with a laugh.

Levi promised he would, but as he entered the ring to fight, Cole stood looking over at him with a smirk.

It was a smirk Levi knew all too well. Head back, eyebrows cocked, he'd seen it too many times to count. From his dad. On the bus. It was the smirk people gave him when they didn't believe he could do something. And it was all the motivation Levi needed.

They were introduced to the officials, then told to touch gloves.

Cole flung his glove into Levi's. "Oh, look, it's the kid from Facebook." When Levi didn't respond, Cole laughed. "Going to wipe the mat with you, bro."

Levi glanced back, but Mr. Anderson cut him a stern look. "Focus."

On *fight*, Cole came at him like a bull. He charged, and Levi moved to sidestep it, but Cole was already whaling like crazy. Levi managed to block the blows but was forced out of the ring. He received a warning.

"You *better* run," Cole advised as they broke apart to take their places.

Again, Levi glanced back at Mr. Anderson, pleading for advice. Cole was taking the fight to him, and he wasn't sure how to reverse the momentum.

On the next clash, Levi tried to keep him at a distance, but Cole blitzed from the start. Levi blinked, and his opponent was on top of him, his fists thumping the side of his head until they were separated.

Mr. Anderson motioned for him. "You're letting him dictate. Stop. Don't let him control the tempo. Do what you do."

Levi nodded, unsure what it was he did or how to do it. The motivation from earlier had fled the ring as he took his place, his mind reeling and his balance off as he tried to gauge his opponent's next move. Then something caught his eye–Noah and Jeremiah were in the crowd. Noah had that perma-smirk on his face. Jeremiah was pointing and laughing.

It shouldn't have mattered. Of course they would show up to root against him, have a good laugh so they could tease him on the bus Monday. It was what they did. But seeing them there, that close to Mr. Anderson, edging toward the mat and threatening this safe world of karate he'd discovered, something broke free inside of him.

"Levi," Mr. Anderson said, pointing to his temple. "Get your head in the fight."

Levi's head had left the fight. His body too. He wasn't controlling anything now, as he lined up, bouncing on the balls of his feet. Across from him, Cole set his fists, ready to come charging in, and this time, Levi would rely solely on instinct.

He closed his eyes. When he opened them, Cole came at him with gritted teeth and eyes blazing. Levi crouched, checked, raised his leg, and snapped a lead round kick to the kid's face.

Cole dropped to the mat. A boom of cheers erupted in the mall. Mr. Anderson yelled something at him, but it was all background noise. Levi stood in position, expressionless, ready for the next round as his opponent slowly got to his feet and shook off the blow he'd absorbed.

Ms. Fleming looked over her fighter and exchanged a glance with Mr. Anderson. Cole nodded his head and stomped back to the center of the ring. Levi wasn't smiling, wasn't ready to celebrate. He was in position, ready to fight.

Cole was no longer smirking. The blow to the head left him angry, but also timid and hesitant. Now inside his opponent's head, Levi went on the offensive.

The next clash, Levi stormed in, a quick fake before cocking his leg like he was going to strike with another kick. When Cole backed off, Levi rushed him with a flurry of punches, landing a barrage of one, two, three, then a fourth strike to the head.

Cole was beaten already. Levi wasn't overconfident, but he could sense it on the mat. But Noah and Jeremiah were still watching, and Levi wanted to make a statement. For all the times they'd bullied him and Gina on the bus, all the times they'd laughed at him. No longer invisible, Levi wanted to show everyone what he'd been holding back.

At *fight*, Levi backed off then crouched. He checked, faked a blitz, and closed the distance between him and his opponent. Cole, who was backing off, adjusted and stepped in to strike.

Levi had been practicing kick after kick, so when he decided in a split second to forgo all sparring techniques and combine everything he'd learned into a flashy display of athleticism and showmanship, the back leg roundhouse kick was merely a decoy. And just as he hoped, Cole was thrown off by the technique, giving Levi the opening he needed.

A quick step and he planted his foot. Levi leaped, his adrenaline carrying him high into the air, until he seemed to be flying as one leg came across, pulling the other around as he spun in mid-air and connected with a perfectly executed tornado kick.

It was over in an instant. Again, his opponent went to the mat as Levi stood in the center of the ring, somewhat surprised at what he'd just pulled off. Judging from the silence in the mall —the only sound a clatter of a phone someone dropped— everyone was stunned, for one, two, three seconds, before the cheers rang down like an avalanche.

Mr. Anderson stood with a blank expression. Ms. Fleming knelt to console her fighter. And there was Gina, who Levi didn't think was going to make it, with the phone in place, already watching the replay as she'd captured the entire incident. Noah and Jeremiah stood stock still with matching expressions of shock and bewilderment.

Once Cole was on his feet, he graciously touched gloves with Levi. "What the heck was that?" he said, but no longer with the cockiness he'd shown before their match.

Levi shrugged, and they bowed to the officials as he was declared the winner.

He was headed to the championship round to face the winner of the next fight between Diego and a boy named

Hunter from Pine Bluff. Levi took his helmet off and smiled. Mr. Anderson motioned for him to come have a talk with him.

Emma, Tony, and Diego smacked him on the back. The judges were openly gushing, how they'd never seen anything like it in a match. Even Kenneth Keaton was congratulating him, holding onto him as Levi got swept up in the crowd, absorbing the praise, still wondering if it was real.

He squeezed through the crowd, smiling, taking it in as he shuffled toward his instructor. He only wished his mother had seen him. Or better yet, his father. Maybe if he had, it would have sent the message Levi had been trying to send all along.

CHAPTER TWENTY-SEVEN

Mr. Anderson struggled to keep composure. When the kid pulled it off, his first reaction was to grab the sides of his head and scream. It wasn't that he'd never seen the kick, he'd done it. But he'd certainly never seen it done in such fashion before today.

If he was being honest, Mr. Anderson had to admit he couldn't have pulled it off. Or maybe he could, if he had ten or twenty times to try it. But he hadn't taught the kid anything like it, the kid had put the combo together himself. And the form, the flash—what made it so impressive—had been something straight from a movie set.

Still, the kid was showing off, and Mr. Anderson was torn between praise and coaching. He couldn't get flashy in the middle of a tournament. Then again, wasn't that why they were there? To show what they had? To recruit? What better recruiting tool than the kid, out there flying through the air with kicks like that, in front of Kenneth Keaton, no less?

Now the kid was getting mobbed. Rightfully so. Mr. Anderson decided to take a breath and let him have his moment. He held back what he'd planned to say, to advise him not to go for low percentage, flashy points. Do the techniques, the fundamentals.

Before he could even get to Levi, Kenneth had squeezed in like a snake. He'd tousled the kid's hair and thrown an arm around the kid like they were old friends.

"Kid. That was something else. Wow, that kick," Kenneth said, shaking his head, wiping the sheen of sweat off his forehead. He looked like he'd been the one out there fighting.

Levi took it in stride, cutting a glance toward Mr. Anderson.

Kenneth noticed Mr. Anderson and they made their way to him. "Well, now I can see why you bet the house on this one. That was amazing. Absolutely amazing."

Mr. Anderson was caught between told-you-so and get your hands off the kid. From the start, Kenneth Keaton had been adamantly against having Levi in the studio, even charging Mr. Anderson for the weapons and gear. Now here he was, taking the kid in like he was the golden goose.

It wasn't until a few of the sponsors approached that Kenneth got distracted. When he did, Mr. Anderson managed to lead Levi to an auxiliary hallway.

The door shut, sealing off most of the crowd noise from the now busy mall. "Well," Mr. Anderson said, throwing out his hands. "Explain what just happened."

The kid's eyes lit up for a beat before he dropped his head. He knew exactly what Mr. Anderson meant. "The kick?" he mumbled.

Mr. Anderson nodded. "Yes, *the* kick. Again."

The kid swallowed, stared off at the wall like he was counting the cinderblocks. Mr. Anderson looked to the stain on his pants once again as Levi fixed his belt and took a breath to compose himself. "Did you ever get teased when you were a kid?"

Mr. Anderson blinked. He'd brought the kid back there to

instruct, give sparring advice, perhaps teach a lesson and nudge the kid to go with fundamentals and solid techniques. This threw him for a loop. He stared at the kid for five, then ten seconds before the truth won out. "Yes."

Levi's head popped up. His chestnut brown eyes searched the instructor's face until they settled. A silent understanding between instructor and student. Levi looked off. "Then you know what it's like, to get harassed on the bus, shoved, called trash because your clothes aren't cool, or clean, or your hair isn't cut. Because your best friend is a girl. Or, anything, really. Whatever you do, it's never good enough. Until you don't even want to try."

Besides the incident with his father, Mr. Anderson had never heard Levi speak so freely or with such emotion. Mr. Anderson set his back against the wall. A minute passed between them before he spoke. "I was short growing up. Always the smallest kid on the playground. I was bullied constantly when I was younger. Is that what—"

"They were out there, watching," Levi blurted out, gesturing to the door. His eyes went glossy. "They were laughing at me. And I just," he stopped, choked with emotion. He shook his head, his voice a whisper. "For once, just this one time, I wanted to see how it felt to control a situation. Isn't that what you told me to do?"

Mr. Anderson was torn between karate and compassion. As an instructor, it was his job to mentor, teach the basics and guide his students along as they grew. And he had done that with Levi. But sometimes they just needed someone to listen. To understand.

"It is, Levi. When you said they were out there, you mean the kids giving you a hard time? The bullies? They're here?"

Levi nodded, wiped his eyes.

Mr. Anderson took it in. "Well, not to make light of the situation, but I doubt they will be harassing you from now on."

The kid almost smiled. Then he was pacing again, his bare feet slapping the worn hallway. "I wasn't trying to hurt Cole. Honestly, I wasn't."

"No, I believe you. He's okay. And hey, I think you finally convinced Kenneth Keaton you're worth having around."

This time Levi did smile.

Mr. Anderson couldn't help himself. "You're an amazing kid, Levi. Both on the mat and off. I'm really proud of you."

Mr. Anderson wanted to give the kid some space. But when he turned to head out, the kid launched into him with a hug. Mr. Anderson hugged him back, and Levi buried his face in his side, his chest convulsing. Mr. Anderson set his hand on his head. "Hey, it's okay. All right. It's okay."

On the other side of the door, the crowd cheered as someone scored a point. The kid pulled away and sniffled. "Sorry, just...sorry."

Mr. Anderson knelt. He looked into Levi's shiny eyes. Not for the first time, he hoped his own son would have even half the heart of this kid standing before him. "No need to apologize. Got it?"

Levi nodded, wiped his face with his sleeve, sinking back into his shyness.

Mr. Anderson tousled his hair. "Now, I'm supposed to be coaching Diego at the moment. Let's go see if he's doing all right without me."

They had started out the door when Levi looked up. "Hey, if Diego wins, who are you coaching when we fight?"

"Hmm, good question."

CHAPTER TWENTY-EIGHT

As it stood, Mr. Tabb was doing an excellent job with Diego, who was up 2-0, when Levi and Mr. Anderson exited the auxiliary hallway and made it back to the mat.

Gina approached. "Holy crap, dude. That helicopter thing you did." She twirled her fingers around. "Um, I didn't know you could fly."

Levi laughed. "I didn't either. Thanks for coming."

"Yeah, I had to blackmail my sister. Anyway, I've got a ton of footage," she said, tapping her phone. "Oh, and did you know our two favorite bozos are here?"

When she looked up to Levi, her smile fell. Levi turned away and wiped his eyes. Mr. Anderson and Levi exchanged glances. Gina started to say something else but stopped.

With a shake of her blue hair, she got back to her phone. "I mean, don't take this the wrong way, but I had no idea you were that good. Like, seriously, dude. They are never going to mess with us again."

Levi smiled. "Really?"

"Yes, really," she said, then held out her phone. "Here, have a look at yourself."

Diego won his match, setting the stage for an all Maple Ridge finals. Ms. Fleming introduced herself to Levi as he was warming up.

"Well, I've heard a lot about you, and I must say, you certainly lived up to the hype."

Levi wasn't sure how to accept the flood of compliments coming his way. "Thanks," he said, his cheeks warm. He was caught between asking about Cole and not wanting to bring it up.

The crowd had now swelled past the seats as he took the mat to face off against Diego. Sure, Levi was still nervous, but in a good way. After the kick, and making it to the finals, it felt like he had nothing to lose. He'd proven he belonged.

Kenneth Keaton was beaming at him from the front row, and as he and Diego tapped gloves, Diego shot him a grin. "No video game moves."

Levi smiled, until Mr. Anderson reminded him to focus. Across the mat, Mr. Tabb coached up Diego. Levi started bouncing. He was still wishing his mom could be there, to watch him fight and see how everyone had mobbed him, but she could always watch the videos. He was almost smiling again when he glanced over to his left and found a broad figure amongst the shoppers, with his arms crossed over his chest. Levi stopped bouncing. It was a figure Levi recognized all too well.

A gut punch. The air left Levi's lungs, and he almost collapsed to the floor. What was his dad doing here?

Diego scored quickly. Levi never saw the punch. He'd already been knocked out by the shock of his father watching, lurking in the weeds. Mr. Anderson called time. Levi hobbled over to his instructor in a daze.

"What's going on? You win a few matches, and you can't focus?" He was half joking, but Levi was sealed off, the blood draining from his face.

He tried to swallow the fear down. He cut his gaze back to the crowd.

Mr. Anderson gripped his arm, which by then was visibly shaking. Concern washed over the instructor's face. "Hey, hey. Levi. What's going on?"

Levi wanted to point to his dad, ask Mr. Anderson to protect him. But he couldn't speak, couldn't lift his arm. Besides, how could he keep asking Mr. Anderson for favors, big and small? Free karate, free gear, free tournaments. Free around the clock security.

He did his best to speak, his voice scratchy and hoarse. "Sir. I'm so sorry, but I have to go."

Mr. Anderson's eyebrows flew up. "Go? Go where? Levi, look at me. Is it the bully kids we talked about?"

"No," he said, although it was pretty much a lie, because the biggest bully he'd ever met stood in the crowd, still watching him from across the mall.

The official asked if everything was okay. Mr. Anderson asked for another minute. Diego, across the mat, stood in full gear, his hands at his sides, waiting for Levi to come out and fight him. Only there was no fight left inside of him. It was gone.

His hands were trembling too hard to get his gloves off.

Mr. Anderson noticed. "Hey, you're shaking. And your face is gray. Levi, look at me."

The official came over to check in again, and Mr. Anderson told him they were going to have to forfeit. Diego threw his hands out in frustration. Kenneth Keaton was out of his seat.

Levi tried and failed to look Mr. Anderson in the eye. "I have to go. I can explain later, I promise."

Levi managed to scan the crowd, and once again he found his father, now openly staring at him.

Mr. Anderson turned and looked over his shoulder,

following Levi's gaze. "Oh," he said with a sigh. He motioned for Mr. Tabb to come over, and Ms. Fleming.

"Start the demos."

"What? We did the demos."

"Do them again. Have Emma and the team come out. We've got other things happening."

As his father slid through the crowd, Levi's entire body convulsed with fear and shame. But fighting to break free from those familiar feelings was a smoldering rage that took hold in his chest. He was in the championship round, and his father was ruining everything. Would it always be like this? Every time he or his mother tried to climb out of the hole, would his father be waiting to knock them down again? Levi's breaths picked up and the smoldering caught fire.

It had to stop. Right now. The same way he'd used Noah and Jeremiah's presence to fuel his victory, the fire inside Levi spread. He was ready to face his biggest fear.

Levi spoke up. "No, sir. I want to fight."

Mr. Anderson glanced around. "Levi, you're in no shape to fight right now."

Closing his eyes, Levi bit down on his lip. He reeled in his breathing and shook his head, worked to gain control over his emotions. "I can do this. I'm not letting him take this from me."

Levi looked to his instructor without blinking. Like in the hallway earlier, they held each other's gaze.

Mr. Anderson nodded. "Okay." Then, to the officials, "We're good. If it's okay, we'd like to continue."

After some commotion with the judges, Levi was in the ring again. Diego stood before him. Levi breathed deeply. His father was there somewhere, lurking, watching him. And all he wanted to do was turn his head and scream, but he didn't. He wouldn't. He'd worked too hard to get here. Now it was time to show his father what he could do.

Diego came kicking. Long and fast and like he had four legs. Levi managed to block them as they came, instinctively. And with each one, his confidence soared. It was no longer about karate or his opponent or even his father. It was about him. And nobody was going to take this from him.

His first point came on a simple side kick. His second on a reverse punch. Levi used the defensive techniques taught to him at sunrise in a rippled parking lot. No flash, all fundamentals, as though he were proving a point to Mr. Anderson, or anyone else. He could win in all sorts of ways. He was deliberate, determined, and dangerous. In fact, he was glad his father was there now. This would serve as notice.

Diego scored on a hook kick. But during the next round, Levi sidestepped, faked, then turned his entire body to pivot and land a perfect roundhouse to Diego's temple.

The tournament was over. Levi had won first place.

It was only a mall tournament. Only two schools competing. But it was everything to Levi as he lifted the shiny trophy high over his head. To him, he was hoisting a banner that read, *All of you misjudged me.*

He was still clutching the trophy, Gina catching it all with her phone, when his father approached, clapping his hands.

"Well, look here, I didn't think you had it in you."

Whatever composure Levi had held gave way. His voice broke as he yelled. "What are you doing here?"

Diego, holding a second place trophy, turned to him.

Gina set the phone down. "Come on, Levi. Heather can give us a ride home."

His father stepped closer. "He's coming with me." Then, towering over Levi. "Let's go celebrate."

"I'm not going with you," Levi said, backing away.

"Hey, now you watch your mouth. I told you we were going to start spending time together."

Mr. Anderson was there in an instant. "Everything all right?"

Levi's father puffed his chest out, shoulders square as he used every bit of the three or so inches he had on the instructor. "Between me and my son here."

Mr. Anderson looked at the man but spoke to Levi. "We're going to take a group pic. Come on, Levi."

Levi turned away, but his father reached out and got a hold of the trophy. Levi hung on but got pulled back by his father's force. His dad lowered his head. "Take the pic, then we're leaving."

"Let go of me. I'm not going with you."

Again, Levi tried to move away, but his father tightened his grip. "Levi."

Another jerk and the trophy snapped in two. The small figure fell to the floor.

Levi froze, staring at the broken piece of trophy, his father still grumbling about coming with him.

Mr. Anderson stepped in between them. "We can sort this out later. For now, I think it's best you leave."

Mr. Tabb arrived at Mr. Anderson's side. Ms. Fleming and Diego as well, almost forming a wall of support for Levi, who only stared at the broken trophy—the only thing he'd ever won in his life.

A jostling of bodies in the crowd. His father was shaking his head, blaming Levi and everyone else for what had happened. It wasn't until security closed in that he finally backed off.

It was too much. The bodies and faces, the talking and the gasps. Levi had no strength left. He'd given everything he had, fighting both emotions and opponents. Now it was time for flight. With tears streaming down his face, he turned back, slid out through the bodies in the crowd, and sprinted for the auxiliary door.

He continued running. Down the strange hall, away from his father, from Gina, Mr. Anderson. Busting outside, the sun blasted him as he ran past the dumpsters and all the cars, trucks, and people in the parking lot. He ran until his lungs burned, until the sharp pains in his chest caused him to slow down. Then he walked along the busy streets, his eyes stinging from tears and his father's voice still screaming in his head.

It wasn't until he arrived at the restaurant that he looked down to his bare feet, blackened by tar, stained with blood as one of his toes had split open.

His mother took one look at him and dropped a tray of drinks. She ran to him as he collapsed, sobbing in his gi, a tournament champion with nothing left to give.

CHAPTER TWENTY-NINE

Levi's mother moved heaven and earth to find a new place to live. She caught a break when her boss at the restaurant got word of a small house that had just come available for rent. With a little luck, plenty of work, and a loan, Levi and his mother moved into the two-bedroom house with a small fenced-in backyard.

The timing couldn't have been better. And now, two weeks after the tournament, they were moving in. Mr. Anderson lugged a box in from the truck. He found Levi standing in the living room and nodded toward the door. "Saw some kids down the street," he said with a wink. "Maybe you can hand out some free passes?"

"Yes, sir," Levi said, hurrying outside to help unload the truck while his mother tried to manage the piles of boxes on the floor.

The waitstaff from the restaurant took turns hauling in furniture, along with Mr. Anderson, Mr. Tabb, and some of the kitchen guys—now arriving with the last truckload. It had been a day to say the least.

Levi was relieved to be in a place his father didn't know

about, although still embarrassed beyond words about the scene he'd caused at the mall. He had apologized to Mr. Anderson more times than he could count, and every time Mr. Anderson had reminded him it wasn't his fault. The instructor had even offered to replace the broken trophy, but Levi didn't want to replace it, he wanted the one he'd won, which he'd already set on the mantle in the new house, the karate figure now affixed with superglue.

He'd received a hero's welcome at karate class following the tournament. Walking in, Emma led the applause as Mr. Tabb patted him on the back. Mr. Anderson recognized him and Diego and then asked if they were ready to get back to work. And that was that.

It went that way the past two weeks. No one mentioned the thing with his father, only smacked him on the back and called him champ in passing. They trained hard, and Levi basically lived at the studio. If he wasn't at class, he was there for sparring. If he wasn't sparring, he was running circles around the parking lot. If he wasn't training, he was doing his homework in the back or taking out trash, scrubbing mats and cleaning mirrors, usually ducking and weaving along the way, always sparring in his mind.

With the last truck unloaded, Mr. Anderson's phone started ringing. He had to get home, something about pictures with the baby. As though sniffing out that all the heavy lifting had been done, Gina arrived, getting dropped off by Heather, who waved to him from the curb. Levi was still waving as her car putted up the road.

"High school," Gina said with a laugh.

Levi snapped out of his daze.

Gina looked around. "Cool place," she said, taking it in. "Only, now you're walking distance to the school, which leaves me to ride the bus all by myself."

"Sorry," Levi offered.

Gina laughed, shrugging it off. "Don't be. Actually, I don't think our two favorite goons will be messing with us for the foreseeable future."

"Really?"

"Levi, do I need to remind you again that you won a karate tournament?"

"Oh yeah," Levi laughed. "I forgot."

"You forgot. Well, I didn't." She raised an eyebrow. "Wait until you see the next promo."

Gary and Isaac, kitchen guys from the restaurant, scooted up the walkway, hefting a couch. Levi ran to open the door.

"Thanks," Gary managed, as they twisted the couch one way then the other before they slid it into the house.

Gina's eyes softened. "So, you doing okay? With, like, your dad and everything?"

"He's not my dad," Levi corrected. No real dad would show up at a tournament and break their son's trophy, by accident or otherwise. Gina had said how after Levi left, the cops had shown up asking questions, and his dad vanished quickly.

A pull of fear gripped Levi's insides. He decided to change the subject. "I guess we could help Mom."

As great as everything was, with the new house and the backyard, Levi couldn't shake the feeling that his father would eventually find out where they lived and ruin everything. His father had a habit of doing that, finding things out and ruining them. Like he had at the mall.

Something told him it was only a matter of time. His dad knew where his mom worked. He knew where the karate studio was located. So while Levi let himself believe moving would fix all their problems, in reality it probably only gave them a few extra weeks, days even.

But for now, things at home were blissfully quiet. The new

house was not only closer to school, but closer to Crawford Road, and in turn, Kick City. Now Levi wouldn't have to bother Mr. Anderson for rides to the studio for class when his mother worked late, arriving home with leftovers.

It took a few days of getting settled in. But for Levi, the best moment he could remember came on a sunny Tuesday afternoon. It was before karate class, and Levi's mom had the evening off. They were out in the backyard, Levi was practicing moves as his mom was planting tomatoes in a small dirt patch she'd claimed for a garden. It was late in the year for it, but there was no talking her out of trying.

She looked up and the sun hit the side of her face, splashing off her cheeks and causing her to squint. She smiled proudly, watching Levi go through Circle Forms.

"I don't know if I told you how proud I am of you, Levi."

Levi threw a kick, then turned to her. "Thanks, Mom."

She had a smudge of dirt on her forehead as she shook her head, and Levi knew she was about to get all mushy gushy, but then again, they were in their own backyard, and he didn't mind so much. "I'm serious," she continued. "I never thought, when you ran across the street and went to that karate studio, that it would lead to all of this," she said, throwing her hand toward him. *This* meaning everything.

"Me neither," he said, finishing up the form.

"Then you met Mr. Anderson," she continued. "And won that tournament. It's been something."

"Yeah," he agreed, hoping she would stop, but then again hoping she would keep going. It could be worse, she could be telling him to pick up his dirty socks or dishes. Levi could live with his mom telling him how great he was once in a while.

And then it returned, rushing in from the back of his mind. All the questions about his father. His presence loomed in the background, like a passing cloud throwing shadows on an otherwise sunny day. He wanted his mother to tell him it was over for good. Say they were safe. But who could promise such things? And besides, it would only ruin the moment. In Levi's experience, sunny mornings usually led to stormy afternoons.

His mother was still smiling. Digging and smiling. "Well, I'm just so proud of you. And Grandma would be too."

Levi stopped his forms. His mother hardly ever talked about Grandma, who'd passed away suddenly a little over a year ago. In the weeks after the funeral, Levi would hear his mother crying in her bedroom behind the closed door. And while she hadn't done it more recently, Levi knew it still pained her to no end.

She nodded, as though acknowledging what she'd said. "I just wanted you to hear me say it. I know I'm busy a lot, with work, and things aren't always easy, but you're growing into such a young man. I'm—"

"Mom," Levi said with a little laugh.

She got to her feet, shaking off the dirt crumbs as she opened her arms and started for him with a laugh. Levi dodged her once, but then came into her and she hugged him, smearing her garden dirt all over his shirt. He didn't mind one bit. He hugged her tighter.

CHAPTER THIRTY

"Three weeks until the Invitational, and we have lots to cover." Mr. Anderson paced in front of the class. His eyes were like lasers as he stated for the hundredth time exactly what was expected from his students—which was that everyone, all of them, needed to come out and compete. Forms, demos, weapons, sparrers, they were all expected to make the trip.

Levi read between the lines. The mall had been great, but Mr. Anderson needed to show Kenneth Keaton that they were for real here at Maple Ridge. And Levi was with him. Yes, he wanted to win for himself, but he desperately wanted to repay this man for everything he'd done for him.

Classes ran later. The normal sixty minutes stretched to seventy-five, then ninety. Parents shifted in their seats, checking phones and watches. Everything was tight and tense. Beginners were welcome but quickly lost in the shuffle. Mr. Anderson became stingy with compliments, harder to impress. He was sharp, focused, and ready to pounce on anyone not giving their best effort.

Levi wasn't about to be caught slacking. He punched harder, kicked higher. He did forms until he was drenched. Mr.

Tabb called him out in class and had him demonstrate technique. Only Tony occasionally snickered, everyone else knew better.

If class had become intense, Fight Night was a pressure cooker. There was no talking, mostly because everyone was sucking wind. Emma had been noticeably absent since the mall tournament. Tony had taken a break from badgering him. Levi held his own, but every time he fought Diego, he remembered how the fighter had helped him before his first match, when his nerves had the best of him.

Things came to a head when Diego beat Levi three times in a row. Mr. Anderson calmly pulled Levi aside and asked Mr. Tabb to take over. Mr. Tabb stepped in while Mr. Anderson escorted Levi to the chairs in the back of the studio and asked him to have a seat.

He threw his hands out. "Do you want to be here?"

Levi's gaze sprang up from the floor. How could Mr. Anderson ask him that? He was the one person who knew more than anyone there was no place he'd rather be. Levi took a few breaths while Mr. Anderson waited, patiently, so Levi had no choice but to find an adequate excuse. He rolled his arm around. "Yeah, my shoulder..."

Mr. Anderson was already dismissing the excuse. Levi's gaze returned to the mat where Diego was in a match with Darren, a decent sparrer who liked to rush like a bull. Levi must have been staring too long, because Mr. Anderson was onto him. He called out to the floor, "Diego, can you come over here?"

A flush of panic as Levi looked to Mr. Anderson. On the mat, Diego stopped, glanced over to his instructor, and nodded. He jogged toward them.

Levi almost begged his instructor. "What are you doing?"

Mr. Anderson ignored Levi's question as Diego removed his helmet. "Yes, sir?"

Mr. Anderson's eyes never left Levi. "Diego, how would you feel if another fighter 'let you win'?"

Diego's face scrunched up like he had a bad taste in his mouth. He set a glare on Levi. "I would be insulted, sir."

Levi couldn't help the urge to explain himself. "I didn't let him win."

"What?" Diego turned to Levi. "You better not," he said, low and serious.

Mr. Anderson looked at both fighters before his gaze settled back on Levi. "That's not how we operate here."

Levi struggled for words. Ever since the tournament he couldn't shake the nagging guilt over beating Diego. He wished they could both win. Still, Levi wasn't exactly *letting* Diego win, although in the back of his mind he hadn't done his absolute best to score, either.

Mr. Anderson stood straight up, glanced over at Diego. "And he's right, it is an insult. You're actually disrespecting him as a peer and a fighter."

"I didn't—"

Mr. Anderson cut him off. "Okay, you didn't let him win. But giving anything besides your best is doing a disservice to your opponent and yourself. Your heart might be in the right place, Levi, but if you're not competing the way you did in the tournament, it shows a lack of respect toward the other fighter."

Levi nodded. "Okay."

Diego slid his helmet back on. "Well then, rematch?"

Levi smiled. "You got it."

Mr. Anderson raised an eyebrow. "Understand?"

"Yes, sir."

CHAPTER THIRTY-ONE

Mr. Anderson hated asking for handouts. He'd had help along the way, but he'd also put in everything he had to get where he was—a fifth degree black belt with his own karate studio. He took pride in doing what he loved. He had an amazing wife and a healthy baby. He'd brought in this phenomenal kid who found new ways to blow his mind every single day.

But Kenneth Keaton was impossible to please.

Kenneth saw the world differently. Where Mr. Anderson saw a room full of eager students, Kenneth saw memberships, passes, and dues, new ways to squeeze parents for money.

Even after the boost from the mall tournament, Kenneth had not let up about recruiting. Sure, Levi's kicks had stolen the show and bought him some time, but now Kenneth was back to sending emails nonstop about rate increases, class sizes, merchandise, and promotional events. But what set Mr. Anderson off was that he'd docked the studio for Levi's membership fees, then turned around and docked them for his tournament entry fee as well. It was never going to get settled between them. Now it was time to go to the big guns.

Margaret Keaton was Mr. Anderson's only hope when it came to keeping Kenneth in check. While most of the accounting duties fell to her son, the Kick City brand was hers exclusively. She had the final say.

At least it was a nice day for a drive. The sprawling mountains and countryside worked to clear his head, and the fact that the kid had wanted to come made things all the easier.

"Thanks again for driving out with me," he said to Levi, who turned away from his window and nodded. Mr. Anderson wondered what was going through his head. "Sure this is all right with your mother?"

"Yeah, she's closing tonight."

Sometimes Mr. Anderson forgot how much time the kid spent alone. It had been the same for him growing up, how the hours and hours of daylight stretched out in front of him, the days feeling like weeks, months, as his mother slept off her troubles.

He wanted to ask Levi about his father but was careful not to pry. He sat back and drove instead, enjoying the lush green landscape as they got farther away from town.

The houses were spaced farther apart. Mr. Anderson remembered when Master Keaton had bought the land, had the house built, and moved his family out to the country. He said it helped him meditate, being in the trees with the birds and wildlife. Mr. Anderson had thought it was odd at the time, but now, as the sun filtered through the cover of oaks and maples and sycamores, he understood completely.

"One week to go. You think you're ready?"

Levi stared at the dashboard in earnest.

Mr. Anderson had never seen a kid so serious before.

"Do you think I'm ready?" he said, popping up.

Mr. Anderson smiled. An excellent response, and one that deserved an honest answer. "Only one way to find out," he said.

"But if you bring what you've been bringing, fight like you did at the mall—I like our chances."

They pulled in and started up the curling driveway that climbed to the Keaton house. Not a mansion, but not exactly a cabin, either. The sunlight reflected off the floor-to-ceiling windows that made up the front of the house. A large wrap-around porch, complete with rocking chairs, ran along the side. Mr. Anderson watched the kid take it in.

"Cool place, huh?"

Levi nodded.

They stepped out of the car, and Mr. Anderson saw Margaret hunched over, working at the weeds in the yard. He motioned that way, and the kid followed.

"Hello, Mrs. Keaton," he called.

The floppy sunhat turned as the lady stood up and wiped herself clean.

Mr. Anderson smiled at Levi. Seventy-six-years old and she got around like a teenager.

They met in front of the house. Mrs. Keaton smiled at Levi. "Is this handsome young man the one I've heard so much about?"

"Sure is. Levi Rocco. He won the in-house tournament a few weeks back."

"Oh yes," she said, brightening. She removed a glove and offered a hand to Levi, who took it gently.

Mr. Anderson smiled seeing how the kid was blushing.

"So nice to meet you, dear. From what I gather, you've done well for yourself."

Mr. Anderson couldn't help wondering what else she'd heard from her son, who was probably whining about billing costs and tuition. Sometimes Mr. Anderson wondered how Kenneth could be related to people so compassionate as Master Keaton and his wife. But today his goal was to play nice and have a cordial visit. One that did not include thinking or talking about Kenneth Keaton until it was absolutely necessary.

Margaret invited them in for lemonade. As they entered, Mr. Anderson watched the kid marvel over the framed pictures of Master Keaton in action—military, karate, humanitarian causes. He gave the kid a gentle nudge. "Wait until I show you the trophy room."

Margaret led them to a counter that separated the living area from the kitchen. She filled a glass and slid it toward Levi. "Mr. Anderson here has told me all about what you've accomplished in such a short time."

Levi stopped short from sipping. "Well, I just really like karate," he managed.

Margaret smiled, her eyes crinkling as she regarded him.

He was a natural, Mr. Anderson thought, and not just with karate. He was humble and kind. Something everyone in the room could appreciate.

Margaret closed her eyes. "Yes, well, me too."

After a quick tour of the trophy room, Mr. Anderson told the kid he needed a moment to speak with Margaret in private. The kid nodded, still studying the gear, all the framed photos, the shining trophies, soaking the room up like a sponge.

Mr. Anderson found a seat across from Margaret and took in the view from the windows.

She watched him with a smile. "Impressive kid."

"You have no idea."

"Oh, I think I do. He reminds me of someone I know."

It was Mr. Anderson's turn to blush, before he got down to business. "He's remarkable. And he's got this friend, she's some kind of social media whiz. Have you seen the promos?"

"Yes, I thought we paid for those."

Mr. Anderson smiled as he shifted in his seat. He was thankful for the years of endurance training. He needed it to calm his nerves. "With all due respect, to me, Kick City isn't just a business, but a school. For some, it's even more. It's a place to feel safe. A refuge from a world that seems to be getting increasingly harsh. And if I can be honest here, Kenneth doesn't understand what we're trying to do at Maple Ridge."

She nodded at his prepared comments. "You know that I agree with you, Cody."

"This kid," he said, leaning closer, going off script. "He can do it. He can win this tournament. He's a black belt through and through. Maybe even a master. He has it."

He was pleading now, and she turned to look at him full on. "I haven't seen you this worked up in a while."

"I know. Maybe it's having a family of my own now, but it's kids like Levi that are the reason I do this at all." He took a deep breath. "I'd like for his tuition to be waved."

"Completely?" she said, raising an eyebrow. "Like some kind of scholarship?"

Scholarship. Grant. Whatever it took. Mr. Anderson nodded. "Yes. I need Kenneth to back off. I know he wants to expand, and we will. But we have to do it the right way. It's what Calvin did for me."

Margaret looked off to the trees outside. Mr. Anderson couldn't tell if he'd gone too far or not gone far enough, until she turned to him and smiled. "I think you're right, Cody. Calvin would want this." She reached over and patted his hand. "I'll approve it. And let's not worry so much about Kenneth. He's awfully excited about the remodel at Pine Bluff. It is a busy studio. But my heart will always be here, with Maple Ridge."

Mr. Anderson hadn't realized just how badly he needed to hear it until she spoke the words. He set his head down and breathed.

Margaret patted his hand again. "The boy is lovely. And

he's welcome to stay. I'll wave his fees. This stays between you, me, and Kenneth, if you don't mind."

Mr. Anderson looked up and did his best not to leap out of his chair. Instead, he nodded. "Of course."

"It's good to see you this excited again. How's the baby?"

A stab of guilt. Mr. Anderson had been so busy with the studio he hadn't made enough time for his own kid.

Margaret seemed to understand. "Go home. Spend time with them. Kiss your wife and child. You're doing such good work for us, be sure to do it with your family too."

Mr. Anderson bowed his head like he was twelve years old all over again. "Yes, ma'am."

CHAPTER THIRTY-TWO

L evi's entire body was sore from training. His arms hurt, his legs hurt, even his hair hurt as he climbed out of bed on Monday. It was a feeling he'd come to appreciate, if not love.

The burn in his legs eased as he walked from his new house to school, and as he entered the lobby and found Gina on her phone, he smiled.

"How was the walk?" Gina asked, looking him over.

"Good. How was the bus?"

"Oh, just dandy."

"No problems with...?" Levi gestured across the lobby toward Noah and Jeremiah, who glanced up and smiled. Levi drew a quick breath as they started across the room.

"Oh, about that. I think they want to talk to you," she said with a roll of the eyes.

Levi tensed as Jeremiah actually nodded in greeting as he made his way up to them. Behind him, Noah followed with his head down and his hands in his pockets.

Levi frowned at Gina. Their tormentors weren't smirking or ribbing each other as they approached. They almost seemed sheepish as they stopped in front of Gina and Levi.

Jeremiah nodded his head again. "Hey, Levi, what's up?"

Again, Levi looked to Gina for answers. She crossed her arms, making no effort to conceal her distrust.

"Hi," Levi managed. Awkward didn't cover it, standing there with the two boys who'd tortured him every morning all year long, now suddenly trying to strike up a conversation.

"So," Noah began, "just wanted to say that was cool, at the mall. Didn't know you were some kind of ninja." He did a karate chop with his hands. "That was crazy."

"Thanks, but I'm not a ninja," Levi said softly. He stared at the floor.

Gina did not stare at the floor. She took a step toward them. "You're *so* lucky he's a nice guy too. If it were me, I'd kick you both to the moon."

Noah nodded. "Yeah, sorry about all the pranks. We deserve that, I guess."

"Pranks?" Gina scoffed. She stood between Levi and Jeremiah.

Levi wasn't sure how to proceed, watching them hang their heads and grovel.

Finally, Noah nudged Jeremiah, who cleared his throat. "So, we were thinking about signing up at Kick City. Would uh, would your instructor be able to teach us to do that kind of stuff too?"

Jeremiah was clutching a thirty-day pass. It was all too unbelievable, these two, acting so strange, shy, begging him for lessons.

"Yeah, I mean...probab—"

"Not in a bajillion years," Gina blurted out. She seemed to enjoy having the upper hand. "One, you two combined don't have as much talent as Levi's shoelaces. Two, you would probably just take whatever you learned and use it to beat up some kids on the bus. Right, Levi?"

Levi was caught between trying to recruit and having his best friend's back. "You could come by and take a class, see how it goes, I guess?"

Gina's mouth fell open. "*What?*"

Noah grinned. "That would be awesome. I mean, that kick you did, that was crazy." He spun around and threw his leg out, trying to mimic the kick.

The bell rang, saving Levi from Gina's wrath. With a huff, she spun around and stormed off. Levi called after her, but Noah and Jeremiah were still going on about how great he was.

At lunch, some kids found Levi outside and asked him to do some demonstration kicks. Soon, a crowd formed, as Levi did some jump roundhouse kicks, spin kicks, a few spinning crescent kicks, and a part of the Circle Forms he'd learned. By the time he was done, lunch was ending. He spotted a shock of blue hair and ran to catch up.

"Gina, wait up."

Gina did not wait up. In fact, she sped up.

Levi hurried to catch up with her. "Hey, what's wrong with you?"

She never stopped, never took the time to look at him. "Nothing. Didn't want to disrupt you and your new *friends*."

"Oh," he said catching his breath. "Wait. Are you upset with me?"

Finally, she stopped. A few kids passed, nodding at Levi, smiling. Some held up high fives or made *hi-ya* karate noises. Gina rolled her eyes. "No, Levi. Not at all. Have fun, bye."

Levi wasn't sure what to say. Here he had spent most of middle school feeling invisible. Now it seemed everyone knew him or wanted to know him. Noah and Jeremiah kept playing up his feats at the mall tournament. Eighth graders approached and told him he was awesome. Everything was upside down, and not so much in a bad way.

He had planned on asking Gina if she wanted to walk to his house but never found her after school. Instead, he grabbed a snack and set out for the studio. He got there a half hour before class, being that the new house was so close.

Walking up to Kick City, Levi could see Mr. Anderson working with a couple of new students. It wasn't until Levi had bowed onto the mat that he saw who it was.

"Hey, Levi," Mr. Tabb called out.

Noah and Jeremiah stood on the mat, wearing crisp white belts, going through the motions with Mr. Anderson. "Looks like we have a couple of new recruits. They said they were friends of yours?"

"Oh," he managed, hung up on the word "friends." They'd spent the entire school year making his life miserable. Still, the studio could use recruits. "Uh, yeah."

A couple things entered Levi's mind. One was how upset Gina had been with him today. Two, how uncomfortable (jealous?) he was watching Mr. Anderson teach Noah how to throw a proper backfist.

Levi fixed his belt as Emma breezed through the door. She stopped to bow, and a few others followed as class was about to begin. Levi tried to focus as he took his place at the black line with the others, and Noah and Jeremiah shouldered in on either side of him, laughing and joking with him as though they'd been best friends all their lives.

"My man," Noah said, offering a high five.

Levi slowly put up his hand. He had a thick knot in his stomach that only tightened as he recalled all the times they'd harassed him on the bus or in the hallway. They'd made fun of his shoes, his hair, his clothes, and Gina, and now, here they were at karate, the one place Levi had to himself. It was all wrong. He'd made a huge mistake inviting them there.

Mr. Tabb took the floor, and Levi tried to focus. He went

through the motions. He threw himself into warm-ups, heaved himself through the pushups and sit ups, as though trying to drown out the confusion and outrace the anxiety settling in his chest.

"Okay, let's pair up for grab defenses," Mr. Anderson said.

With Noah being a bit shorter, he was paired with Emma, usually Levi's partner.

Levi found himself facing Jeremiah. And as much as he tried to put it out of his mind, all he could think about were those mornings the bully had teased Gina or thrown trash or balled up notebook paper at them. Levi swallowed it down and did his best to work the techniques.

While they did a walkthrough of the grabs, slowly, going over the movements, Jeremiah shook his head, whispering to Levi. "This is lame. When are we going to do the cool stuff?"

Levi ignored him, still lost in thought. All those shoulder knocks in the hallways, the shoves from behind. The constant wisecracks, how Noah and Jeremiah used to walk on the back of his shoes. All this was going through Levi's mind when Jeremiah took a hold of his head.

In a blink, Levi threw a blow to the leg. With his attacker stunned, he brought his arm around to Jeremiah's chin and struck with an ax chop before flinging the much bigger kid over his shoulder.

Jeremiah hit the mat like a sack. It wasn't until Levi snapped out of it that he realized the entire class had stopped and everyone was staring.

Jeremiah rolled to his side. "Dude, what in the he—"

Mr. Anderson's voice filled the room. "Levi, a hundred pushups, now."

Levi dropped to the mat. Mr. Tabb checked on Jeremiah, who jerked away and mumbled that he was fine. Levi finished up and found Mr. Anderson staring at him. The instructor placed Levi with Emma and had Noah and Jeremiah work together.

After class, Levi was gathering his things when Jeremiah approached. "What's your problem?"

Levi had no excuse for what he'd done. But in the end, he got to his feet and looked Jeremiah in the eyes. "I'm sorry, I guess I got carried away."

"Yeah," he said. "You did."

He didn't shove Levi or threaten him. And that's when Levi noticed something that hadn't occurred to him all day. The bully was afraid of him.

Noah sauntered over to them and laughed. "Don't be mad, man. Levi is just showing you the ropes, right, Levi?"

Levi pictured Gina in his head, and what she'd make of all this. Both boys waited on him to answer. He shrugged. "Something like that." He went for his bag, to get changed for sparring.

Jeremiah called out to him. "So, you wanna hang out this weekend? Noah is having a PS5 marathon at his house."

Unbelievable. These guys suddenly wanted to be his best friends. Levi shook it off. "No, I've got to train. Thanks, though."

"Oh right, another tournament. Hey, how do we get into sparring?"

Oh no, Levi thought, as Mr. Tabb approached and said, "Well, you are welcome to stay and see what we do. Levi here picked it up faster than most. But if you guys want to learn the basics, we can certainly do that."

The two boys nodded eagerly. "Yes!"

Levi's shoulders dropped. This was not going to go well.

CHAPTER THIRTY-THREE

Something was off with Levi, something that specifically had to do with the two new students. The way Levi had slung the bigger kid to the mat was out of character, and he meant to ask about it the next time he got the chance. But for now, it was time to hunker down and train.

Mr. Anderson directed the fighters to put on their gear. Tony and Levi fought first, and Levi could hardly pay attention. Again, it was clear the two new students knew Levi, and the effect was disastrous. Levi lost 3-1, and the kids oohed and ahhed.

Mr. Anderson was careful. He instructed the kids how "Fight Night" was different than regular karate class, while reminding them first and foremost to always be respectful. As badly as he needed new recruits, he wasn't sure if these two fit the mold. They had the smirks of kids who caused trouble. Still, he owed them a fair shot.

Diego beat Tony, then beat a few others. Mr. Anderson called Levi back into the ring, and the two new students started cackling all over again. Mr. Anderson called Levi over. "You know those two?"

Levi nodded. The distant look in his eyes said it wasn't a friendly relationship.

"Okay, well, you gotta put it away, got it?"

This time Levi lost to Diego, but he was at least present in the ring. He came up short, 3-2, in a rematch, and the taller of the new students yelled, "You suck!"

Topping the list of things Mr. Anderson didn't tolerate was bullying. And the way the two boys were clowning around was bully behavior. Mr. Anderson had enough. "I have some gear, if you'd like to give it a shot?"

Being how they weren't quite students, Mr. Anderson had planned to let them go against each other. But the smaller boy backed off quickly, his eyes wide and his head shaking. The other one, the kid Levi had thrown to the mat, said he'd give it a go.

It just so happened that Emma had returned to Fight Night (she'd actually missed sparring after all) and was in the ring once Mr. Anderson got the taller kid suited up and ready to go. The new kid nodded at her, smiling like a wolf at dinner time. Mr. Anderson reminded him of how it worked. Backfists and reverse punches. The kid nodded through it all.

From the first round, Mr. Anderson realized his mistake. The kid attacked Emma, swinging wildly and pounding away. Emma stumbled back, her hands over her head as the kid pummeled her like he was in a street fight.

"Okay, stop. Enough!" Mr. Anderson called out.

The taller boy stopped slugging Emma and turned around.

"Jeremiah, right? We stick to karate moves, here. We're not whaling away, wild and crazy, got it?"

"Just fighting, man."

Mr. Anderson's eyes flashed as he nodded.

Emma was back on the line, still shaken by the attack, when Levi stepped into the ring. "I can show him, if you'd like?"

So these were the bullies from the bus. Mr. Anderson finally put it together. Years of instructing told Mr. Anderson to shut it down and let the experienced sparrers have the mat. But the way Levi stood, his chin out as he stared down the taller boy, the one who'd just called him "man," made it difficult to resist. And so, Mr. Anderson made his second mistake of the night.

"Okay," he said. "Levi, show him the basics." Again, Mr. Anderson instructed the taller boy on how to get in a defensive stance and bounce on his toes.

"Okay, we ready?"

Levi only stared.

Jeremiah nodded. "Bring it on."

At *fight*, Levi pounced.

He didn't fake. He didn't weave or bounce. He shot forward with a skip side kick before launching into a spinning crescent hook kick that clapped the kid in the back of the head.

Jeremiah fell on his face but got up quickly, his cheeks splotchy and red, eyes flashing with anger. Before Mr. Anderson could intervene, Jeremiah bull rushed Levi, who was ready and waiting with his guard up, poised to strike again.

Levi blocked Jeremiah's wild punches in sequence with his high guard before executing two swift shots to the kid's midsection, folding him like an accordion.

The kid fell to his knees. His teeth clenched, he shot a hard glare at Levi. "You're dead."

"Enough!" Mr. Anderson took the ring. Again, Levi was in a ready position. Mr. Anderson waved him back and spoke to the visiting student. "A few things. One, don't ever threaten one of my students again. Do you understand?"

Jeremiah ripped off his gloves and threw them to the floor. The helmet came next and then the foot pads. "Whatever, dude. I'm out of here."

Jeremiah stepped toward Levi once again but stopped cold

seeing Levi set in advanced guard, his fists clenched and his face a block of stone, nothing but hot glaze in his eyes.

Diego, Tony, Emma, and Devin fell into place beside Levi.

Jeremiah took a breath before he wiped his eyes. "Screw this," he said, shaking his head. "I'm out of here." He pointed at Levi. "Wait until we catch you alone."

"I'll be ready," Levi said, fists up, still in his fighter's stance.

The two boys stomped for the door, Jeremiah loosening the white belt, which he yanked from his waist and tossed to the floor as he stomped out. "This place is a joke. Come on, Noah."

Noah didn't look so sure about giving up his new white belt. Eventually he did as he was told, and the two stormed out of Kick City.

Only then did Levi break his stance. He rushed over to pick up the belts and brought them to Mr. Anderson. "I'm sorry, sir."

Mr. Anderson watched the two boys stomp off. "Those are the kids who've been giving you trouble? The ones from the tournament, right?"

Levi nodded. "Yes, sir, but I'm not worried about them. Not anymore."

Mr. Anderson held back a smile. The kid's demeanor had changed in an instant, from hardened fighter back to the shy smile. Mr. Anderson bent low and looked Levi in the eyes. "Just remember, it's one thing to stand up for yourself and others. But never let yourself become the bully, you got that?"

Levi nodded. "Yes, sir. I'm sorry."

"Don't be," he said, patting him on the back. Mr. Anderson looked around at his fighters with a swell of pride at how they'd stood together. "Okay, new students are welcome. But only students with positive attitudes will be invited to stay. That said, where were we? Let's fight."

CHAPTER THIRTY-FOUR

In the days leading up to the Invitational, Kick City was all business. Everyone put in a bit more, threw every kick and punch with purpose. The lights came on as the school stayed open later. There was less smiling and chattering as the reps became grueling. And it wasn't just the fighters.

The demo team was training like Mr. Anderson had never seen before. Emma was leading the way with a full somersault kick combo that she was determined to get right.

Mr. Anderson's hands hurt from clapping. He couldn't have been prouder of his students. From the nun chucks flying, to the sparrers locked in battle, and the demo team all synched up and moving as one. And then it all came to a halt, as Kenneth Keaton breezed through the door.

Kenneth stopped momentarily, waiting for safe passage across the mat. It certainly was something to see, everyone working together, lost in a love of martial arts, but as Mr. Anderson had learned long ago, Kenneth Keaton wasn't concerned with comradery or unison. He was only interested in the numbers that filled his spreadsheets. Eventually, he found a way over to Mr. Anderson.

"Need to speak with you," he said, as though the instructor wasn't busy.

Mr. Anderson ignored him. "That's it, Tony. But pivot as you come through, use your hips to turn that ridge hand."

Kenneth Keaton cleared his throat. It would have been comical if it weren't so irritating, him popping up out of the blue. He motioned toward the back. "Cody. I need to speak with you."

It would have been fun to continue ignoring the little man. Mr. Anderson had, after all, already secured Margaret's blessing. Then again, maybe that was the reason he was there at all. Eventually, he turned to Kenneth. "Oh, hi, Kenneth," he said. Then, because he couldn't resist, he added, "Did you come to fix that leaky faucet in the bathroom?"

Mr. Tabb snorted.

Kenneth's lips tightened. "No. I came to talk about memberships."

Mr. Anderson would rather have his teeth pulled than talk memberships. Just then, Levi scored on a soaring jump roundhouse. The room erupted, drawing the ire of Kenneth's stare.

"Let's start with that one. Are you picking up his tab? His thirty days have come and gone. Twice."

"Not sure if you can tell, Kenneth, but we're awfully busy prepping for the invitational tournament. Is there something you need, or can I focus on my students?"

"We can talk in the back," Kenneth Keaton said, gesturing for the office door.

Mr. Anderson nodded to Mr. Tabb, who raised an eyebrow in a show of sympathy.

Once in the office, Mr. Anderson shut the door, sealing off the sounds of feet on the mat, of punches being thrown. Of sparring and weapons and all the things he loved so much.

"Okay, I thought we had a deal," Mr. Anderson said, unable to hold it back any longer.

Kenneth Keaton was already settling into the worn office chair. He logged into the ancient desktop and clicked around until he found a spreadsheet. "You don't honestly think this kid will win the invitational tournament, do you?" The chair squeaked as he turned around, drumming on the arm rests.

Mr. Anderson resisted the urge to roll him and the chair out back and off the loading dock. "Yes. Did you not see him at the last contest?"

Kenneth turned back to the screen. "Small potatoes. This is the big one, all the studios. There's a kid in Pine Bluff who—"

"You know, for someone who loves Pine Bluff so much, you sure do spend a lot of time down here with us. Besides, we beat them head-to-head, remember?"

Click clack went the keys. Where Kenneth could hardly put one foot in front of the other, he was a whiz on the keyboard. "You know, Cody. I'm only trying to prepare you for what's coming. Have you seen that new place across town, the Karate Palace? Place was packed to the gills. Listen, I know you love what you do here, but we need to think about the future. Have a look."

Mr. Anderson had heard about the new place, but it was across town, out of mind. Reluctantly, he eased forward as Kenneth presented the screen, full of dizzying numbers, data, different calculations that crossed the instructor's eyes. Through the maze of colors, one thing was clear. Maple Ridge was coming up last. Last in membership dues, last in number of students. Last in thirty-day passes. Last. Last. Last.

Mr. Anderson's legs went weak.

Kenneth sat back, happy to have the upper hand. "So, yes. We still have a deal. If that boy wins, he can stay on. But if he loses, things are going to change around here. Big time."

Mr. Anderson had his secret weapon: Margaret's word that the kid could stay no matter what. Still, it was hard to look at Kenneth—with his numbers and spreadsheets and talk of change—and not feel a little queasiness in his stomach. Besides, this was Mr. Anderson's livelihood. He shouldn't make wagers that jeopardized his family. But every time Kenneth Keaton came crashing into the studio unannounced, it drove Mr. Anderson to the brink of destruction.

Regardless of the data, the kid had a chance, and that was enough for him. Besides, what was done was done.

Wobbly legs beneath him, Mr. Anderson stood up straight and patted Kenneth on the back. "Great job with the numbers, Kenneth. Really. But the kid will win." Mr. Anderson turned for the door. "Now if you could go take a look at that faucet, I have a class to teach."

That night, as Mr. Anderson walked into his house a little after ten, it felt much later. All the lights were off, and everything was quiet. He set down his bag and made his way to the baby's room. Peeking in, he heard the raspy breaths of his son sleeping. He listened for a while, not daring to step closer, fearing he'd wake the baby up, but enough to breathe in the baby smells and synch his heart with the small boy's sleepy breaths.

After a quick shower and a change of clothes, he pulled the covers back and scooted close to Marissa.

She snuggled into him. "Where've you been?"

"Training with Levi."

Marissa rolled over.

Mr. Anderson set his arm around her shoulders. "Kenneth came by again."

"That explains why you're so stressed."

"I'm not stressed."

"You are. I'm lying next to a block of granite."

"And then I drove by that new place. The Karate Palace."

Marissa turned back over. "I'm sorry, *what?*"

Mr. Anderson wasn't sure what to say. He couldn't explain why he'd gone to scope out the competition across town when he should've been driving home. It was a bad move. From the parking lot, he'd looked on at the well-lit room, clean and bright with brand new equipment. It was Kenneth Keaton's dream. And what made things worse, the place was still packed at nine at night. At least twenty kids in there, lined up with new gis. It was like a punch to the gut.

"Cody, I know you have a lot of stress here recently, with the tournament and all, but do you honestly think that's a good way to spend your time?"

"No."

Marissa took his hand. "I thought you spoke to Margaret, that everything was fine."

"It is, I think. It's just that, that place is brand new, it's bright and shiny, and they had so many kids in there. I just want to teach karate, not do all of...this."

She took breath in the dark. "I know, sweetheart."

"But if Levi wins this tournament, it will show Kenneth and Karate Palace and everyone else what we can do. What I do. That substance is more than flash. It will prove that my way can work, make a difference. Isn't that what I'm trying to do?"

Marissa went quiet.

Mr. Anderson stared up at the ceiling. He didn't need any light in the room to read her face.

She gave his hand a squeeze. "It is, Cody. Don't question it."

Mr. Anderson turned to his wife.

She rested her hand on his cheek. "But, what if he doesn't win?"

"He will."

"But you have to be prepared for that. If he doesn't win, it doesn't mean you aren't a good teacher. You've only had this kid for a few months. You can't realistically expect him to go win tournaments. Not state tournaments, anyway."

"You're right."

Marissa flopped over. Five seconds later she flopped back over, reading him in the dark. "But?"

"But I do."

CHAPTER THIRTY-FIVE

Levi missed his best friend's sarcastic comments. He missed her quick wit and spunky sense of humor. Mostly he missed her unwavering support. With that in mind, he woke up early and hiked to his old bus stop.

Coming down the hill, he smiled as he saw his friend—her hair now completely pink. His chest tightened even as something loosened at the same time.

"I like your hair," he said in way of greeting.

Gina glanced up from her phone, her eyes widening before they fell back to the screen. "Are you lost, or...?"

"Yeah, no. Maybe," he said.

Gina stuffed the phone in her back pocket and crossed her arms. "Let me guess, you came to hang out with your new best friends?"

"No. Well, half right. I came to hang out with my one best friend."

She almost smiled, then drew it back. "Did you walk all the way over here?"

"Yeah. Well, I jogged. Part of my training."

"Oh, right," she said, her voice losing some of its gruff.

"Man," he said, talking fast, playing catch up. "You're never going to believe what happened. So Noah and Jeremiah showed up at Kick City the other day, and—"

"Oh yes. I've heard all about it."

"You have?"

Gina laughed. "Yeah, those two idiots are telling people they're almost black belts."

"What? They got booted out of Kick City." He relayed the real story about sparring, the familiar neighborhood cars coming and going. It was great to hear her laugh and playfully shove him away when he told her about kicking Jeremiah in the head.

"Wow." Gina's jagged bangs fell to her brow. "I had no idea they came to *your* studio. Yesterday they were talking about another place. Karate Palace or something."

Levi's stomach dropped. "That new place?"

Gina bit her lip. "Yeah, I think so."

Right on time, the bus came over the hill.

"They go to *Karate Palace* now?"

Gina shrugged, hefting her bag. "That's what they said. Probably lying through their teeth."

Levi's stomach dropped as he hiked the steps onto the bus. If this was true, it meant that, jerks or not, he'd chased two more recruits out of Kick City and right into the arms of the competition.

No sooner than they'd taken their seats, Jeremiah was behind them. "Well, if it isn't the two lovebirds."

"Wow," Gina said to Levi, hooking a thumb over her shoulder. "How original is this guy?"

Noah hovered behind his friend, although he wasn't smirking like Jeremiah, who seemed to be in a much better mood than he'd been in the other day. Levi continued to ignore them, right up until Jeremiah plucked the back of his ear.

Levi whirled around, and it wasn't until the last second that he was able to compose himself in time to remain in his seat.

Jeremiah scooted away. "You really think you're something now, huh?"

This time Gina whipped around. "He has nothing to prove to you. Besides," she said with a grin. "I heard you already dropped out. How sad."

"I didn't drop out. That place was loser city." He nodded to Noah. "We joined Karate Palace. The instructor there is a ninja, not some fake, like yours."

Levi gripped the seat tightly, determined not to lose his cool. But Jeremiah was crossing a line. "Don't talk about Mr. Anderson." He wasn't yelling, but his voice was firm.

It worked. Noah slid back while Jeremiah did his best not to show the fear that widened his eyes. "Whatever, man."

"Just ignore him," Gina said.

"Yeah, listen to your girlfriend."

Levi took a deep breath to calm himself, still staring Jeremiah down. "I'm not scared of you."

"Whatever," Jeremiah said, eyes darting away, muttering under his breath as the bus driver called for them to take their seats.

Levi stared them down until Jeremiah blinked and backed away with a laugh. Gina took Levi's arm and they turned around in their seat.

Noah and Jeremiah didn't say another word to Levi for the rest of the day. In fact, they seemed to avoid him the rest of the week. For the first time that year, Levi didn't fill his school day worrying about the kids on the bus. Although, just to be sure, he continued to jog over to Gina's bus stop as part of his training for the tournament that weekend.

Gina recorded three more videos of Levi doing kicks and throwing punches and posted them on the Kick City socials. On

Thursday, Mr. Anderson told him this would be the last practice, and the next two days would be more relaxed for the students to rest and focus. Levi did not want to rest. He wanted to train. He wanted to be prepared and ready.

And he wasn't the only one.

Levi knew Mr. Anderson had a lot riding on the tournament. He wasn't sure exactly what was happening between Kenneth Keaton and his instructor, but it was something big. How they were always talking in private, in the back room. How Mr. Anderson always left the office after those talks looking like he wanted to use the wall for a breaking board. But Mr. Anderson never let on to Levi what exactly was going on between them, just that he was to train and do his best.

Again, Levi vowed to win the tournament; to repay the man who'd done so much for him.

CHAPTER THIRTY-SIX

Levi and Gina sat in a booth at the restaurant where Levi's mother worked. Levi was trying to do his homework, but the tournament—two days away—was like a neon sign in his brain that refused stop flashing. He managed to put it out of mind only when a steaming hot plate of fajitas made it to their table.

"Compliments of the chef," the waitress said with a smile.

Gina wasted no time grabbing a tortilla and scooping the steaming hot peppers onto her plate. Levi's eyes widened as Gina wrapped up the still cooking peppers and went right in with a bite, only to drop the wrap back to her plate. She reached for the water. "Ahhh!" She waved her hand in front of her mouth. "Ouch. Ouch. Oweee."

Levi laughed. "What gave it away, the steam or the sizzling?"

Gina slugged down her water, dribbling some onto her lap. "I couldn't resist."

They were cracking up about it when Levi's mom hurried past their table, winking at Levi in passing. Gina showed off the new promos and videos, then launched into her master plan for a social media blitz after Levi won the tournament. Levi blanched at her confidence in him, but sitting there with his best friend, his stomach full and his books open in front of him, he was about as content as he'd ever been in his life.

He was still nervous about the upcoming weekend, nothing would change that. But he reminded himself that Mr. Anderson had said he was ready. So he took him at his word. Whatever happened would happen. At least that's what he'd tell himself until he got there.

Heather arrived to pick Gina up around eight. Levi worked on his science paper until his mother's shift ended. Finally, a little after nine, she kissed him on the head and asked if he was ready to go.

Since the move, there was a bounce in his mother's steps. Even after a long shift, she smiled at him more. He smiled too. His grades were up. His confidence was soaring. He and his mom had a new home and weren't constantly fighting about a phone or money or school or much of anything. Money was still tight, but his mom seemed to be working toward something.

On the way home, a poppy dance song came on the radio. Levi laughed at his mother's dance moves as they pulled down their street. When she froze suddenly, Levi thought it was part of the routine, until she abruptly turned off the radio and stopped the car in the middle of the street. Only then did Levi see it.

His father's truck sat parked in the driveway. At the house he wasn't supposed to know about. Levi's mind refused to believe it was happening. Maybe it was someone else's truck. The landlord had a truck, didn't he? One of the kitchen guys?

No, it was his father all right. He was leaning against the tailgate.

"Mom, should we..."

Levi was about to suggest they keep going, drive away, turn

around and get back to the restaurant, when his mother's eyes hardened. Her jaw clenched and soon the engine revved, and Levi was thrown to the right as she flung the car into the driveway, stopping only a few feet from the figure at the tailgate.

She threw open the door and leaped out of the car. "How dare you show up here!" Her voice was torn and wrenched, like a rusty nail being pulled from a stud.

Levi was still stuck to the seat, the seat belt still buckled, as all the good feelings, the music and dancing, the smell of fajita's, leaked out of the car and into the night.

When his father lunged for her, Levi screamed at the windshield. His father yelled down at her, almost into her, with so much force it blew her back a step. His father's arms flailed as he screamed about them moving, how they couldn't leave him behind. About money and rights.

Levi heaved himself into action. He unbuckled the seatbelt and opened the door. He forced himself to step out of the car, while his father continued to rage, the veins on his forehead bulging, his arms flying with clenched fists that were closing in on his mother. He grabbed her by the arm, and she tried to break free, but he jerked her one way, then flung her forward. She tumbled to the ground with a shriek.

"Stop it!"

Levi's mom scrabbled to her feet. "Levi, get inside. Now."

Once again, Levi was stuck, caught between his mother and father. His father turned and came for him, eyes wild and wobbly. Levi's ears rang out with panic as his father demanded Levi get in his truck. "You're coming with me. We're going to my place for the night."

Levi planted his feet. "No, I'm not."

His mother took a step, trying to fend him off.

Again, Levi's father shoved her down before he turned to Levi. "I told you to get in the truck," he snarled.

His eyes were mean. His face was washed red with fury. Levi forced himself to face him, to put away the images from the Med First Center. His mom, wearing a brace. How the bruises went from blue to black to a faded yellow. Levi never wanted to see those bruises again, never wanted to read another golf magazine while he waited for his mother in another hospital lobby. So when his father reached for him, Levi was planted and ready. He saw no choice but to react.

The kick caught his father in the jaw. His neck snapped back, and he fell hard between the two parked cars in the driveway. Gravel crunched under Levi's feet as he bent his knees and got into position, his mother sobbing behind him. Tears blurred his vision. He stayed ready, in his right side guard, even as he was living out his worst nightmare.

Levi's father rolled over, one hand on his head as he struggled to get up. "You've done it now, boy."

A quick glance over his shoulder. Levi's mother fumbled with her phone.

His father staggered as he got himself off the ground. He wiped his mouth and spit on the driveway. "You."

Levi held his defensive guard. "Leave us alone."

His father came at him again, but Levi swatted his hand away. They got turned around, and his dad smiled—a lopsided, devilish smile—before he charged him like a bull, just the way Tony had in sparring. Levi saw it coming and sidestepped him, using the much larger man's momentum to throw him onto the hood of the car.

He let out a grunt, then a moan, as he slipped to the ground where he balled up, writhing in pain.

Levi was still staring at his father, wondering what he'd just done, when his mother took him by the arm. "Come on," she said, and led them to the door, fiddling with the keys, her hands shaking as she got the key in the doorknob.

Once they were inside, she locked the deadbolt. Levi's strength drained from his body, and he slumped in front of the window, still keeping a watch on the crumpled figure in the driveway. He couldn't stop his hands from shaking.

"Levi, are you okay?"

Levi didn't realize his mother was standing over him, stroking his head, her shallow breaths colliding with his own. Levi nodded. "I think so. You?"

Minutes later, a police cruiser pulled up to the curb. Then another one. Officers stepped out of the cars, one coming to the front door, another toward his father in the driveway.

His mother took him in her arms, sobbing. "I'm so sorry, Levi. I'm so, so sorry."

It took forever to sort things out. Across the street, neighbors were out in their yards trying to see what the fuss was all about. A third cruiser arrived, then a tow truck, but in the end, Levi's father was helped up only to be cuffed and set in the back of a squad car. Levi heard one of the officers talking about warrants for his arrest—check fraud, trespassing, and other charges coming his way. His mother was teary-eyed as she nodded along, answering questions from the officers. Then they were speaking to him, asking him questions.

An officer said it was commendable, how he'd protected his mother. The other officers agreed, all of them seemingly amazed that he'd defended himself so well. They said he'd make an excellent officer one day and even managed a few lighthearted jokes about karate.

Levi wasn't in the mood for compliments or laughing. He was lightheaded, nauseous, dizzy from trying to sort out his feelings and what he'd done. He still didn't know whether he was mad at his father for being the way he was, or sad that he would never make things right with him.

It was almost midnight when things finally cleared out. The

cruiser carrying Levi's father was the first to leave. The tow truck took his father's truck and its roving orange lights away from the house. Levi retrieved his bookbag from the car, found the leftovers, and dumped them in the trash. When he returned, his mom brought him in for a hug, still in her waitressing clothes, eyes puffy and red, her makeup smeared.

She kept repeating how sorry she was, that it was over now. She wished she'd done something sooner. Levi hardly heard her at all. He'd only wanted to protect her, and he had. But it wasn't as great as he'd imagined. He knew he would never get the image of his father lying in the driveway out of his head.

CHAPTER THIRTY-SEVEN

The gray skies and gloomy rain was fitting for Friday. It matched the thick fog in Levi's head. He'd spent what was left of the night curled tight in his bed, skirting the edges of sleep, seeing his father's face in the dark any time he came close to dozing off.

His mother wasn't sleeping either. A few times he'd found her silhouette in the doorway, as though standing guard at his bedroom.

He woke up late for school, surprised to find his mother in the kitchen, still in her pajamas, making waffles.

"Don't you have to work?" Levi asked, rubbing his eyes.

His mother shook her head. One look at her and it was clear she was in no shape to go anywhere. Levi imagined he looked the same.

"I thought we could use a mental health day."

It usually took mountains to move before his mother called in to work, and only slightly less for her to allow Levi to miss school. But then, mountains *had* moved, or so it seemed. Levi fell into a seat at the table, and once again tried to sort things out.

There were still piles of boxes lining the wall. They hadn't even finished moving in and he'd found them. *He*, Levi thought. Not some monster in the hills, but his own father.

His mother set a waffle on a plate. She grabbed the syrup and a fork and set it down before Levi. She pushed back his bangs and left her hand on his forehead. "I'm so sorry, Lee."

Levi blinked, trying to relieve the pressure behind his eyes. "It's not your fault, Mom."

"It is. Some of it, anyway." She gripped her coffee cup, staring off at the wall. "I should have done something a long time ago. I always hoped that, somehow..." She shrugged, her face straining against the new tears. Yeah, it was going to be a long, heavy day.

Levi's sweatshirt was made of lead. His legs were filled with wet sand. He stayed on the couch, mostly, staring off at nothing. The house looked different in the morning sunlight, the yard too. He managed to glance out to the driveway, where his father had waited in the dark for them to arrive home, like an ambush.

He remembered going to a football game with his father when he was little. He'd hoisted Levi up on his shoulders so he could see the field better, and Levi had been on top of the world. There had to be some of that man in there still, didn't there?

He watched daytime television with his mother until she suggested he read ahead a few chapters in his novel for English. His mother took some calls, from friends, he could tell, by the way her voice cracked, then another one that was more official, by how her voice gained an edge to it. He heard the word "warrants," again. Prison. His dad's name. "At least we're safe," was said more than once.

It wasn't until afternoon that Levi thought about karate. More specifically, the Invitational.

There was no way he could fight. Not now, not tomorrow. Maybe later, down the road, but he couldn't imagine sparring.

Not when his mind was reeling. Taking a stance would only feel like facing his father. He kept seeing his father coming for his mother in the night. Coming for him. It made him shudder.

Which meant...

No more karate.

Karate was such a part of him now that he couldn't imagine his life without it. But he knew what Mr. Anderson had riding on this tournament, how much Levi still had to prove. And yet, after everything Mr. Anderson had done for him, he couldn't force himself to clench his fists without seeing his father coming for him.

Shaking it off, he looked at the trophy on the mantel. Even glued together, it filled him with pride. He never would've been capable of winning a tournament had it not been for his instructor. And now here he was letting Mr. Anderson down when he needed him most.

Levi's mother walked in the room and found him standing at the mantel, holding the trophy. She stopped and her eyes went soft.

"Mom, I can't... I don't think I can fight tomorrow."

"No, I wouldn't imagine you could."

He looked to the figure on the trophy, throwing the kick. "But Mr. Anderson..."

"Will understand. I'm sure of it."

Last night seemed so long ago. Now the tournament was tomorrow, and Mr. Anderson had no idea what had happened. No one did. He borrowed his mother's phone and texted Gina. Then he fell back into the couch and stared at the ceiling, let his thoughts drift through the fog.

He awoke late in the afternoon to a knock at the door. A blast of pink hair on the other side as he opened up. "Hey," he said, fixing his hair. Behind Gina, Heather's car idled at the curb, Heather working the phone with her fingers.

Gina laughed. "Sorry, we're on the way to a thing at our grandparents' house, but I begged her to swing by here. I'm surprised she even stopped the car. Anyway, how are you doing? I mean..."

"Yeah, just. My dad. He came here last night."

Her smile fell. She cocked her head. "Oh, Levi."

Levi stared at the ground. He blinked a few times and then rehashed the whole story, from the fight to the police, the tow truck and the warrants. Heather beeped the horn a few times, but Gina waved her off.

"Wow, Levi," she said, then launched into him with a hug.

Levi hugged her back.

"I'm glad you're okay," she said into his ear, then, letting go, "I mean, are you...okay?"

"I think so. Maybe." He shrugged again. He wasn't so sure after all.

Another beep of the horn from Heather. Gina shook her head. "Okay, okay, jeez," she yelled back at the car. Then to Levi. "Sorry, my sister is having a crisis. Something about cheer session. Yay."

Levi's gaze never made it past Gina to the car. He was a little embarrassed but overcome with gratitude at the same time. It was nice to have his friend checking on him. Gina hopped off the steps and started walking backward toward her sister's car. "Well, I'll text you later, okay?"

"Yeah." Levi smiled for the first time that day. "Thanks for stopping by."

Another beep. Gina turned around and opened the door. "You are the worst!" she yelled at her sister as she got in the car.

CHAPTER THIRTY-EIGHT

Mr. Anderson pulled into the kid's driveway and parked the truck. He took a minute and looked things over. From what Levi's mother had texted him he almost expected busted windows and yellow police tape around the house. It still didn't make sense to him, how a father could do this to his own son—one as exceptional as Levi, no less.

The kid's eyes widened as he opened the door. "Oh, Mr. Anderson. Sir."

"Hey there, Levi."

Ms. Rocco stood at the edge of the room. And while there may have been no broken windows or yellow tape, the entire house had a solemn feel to it.

The boy opened the door a bit wider. "Do you want to come in, sir?"

Mr. Anderson nodded. "If it's all right."

Levi turned, and Mr. Anderson followed him inside. He folded up a blanket and set it over the couch as Mr. Anderson clasped his hands. There was nothing in a training seminar or workshop that had prepared him for this sort of thing. Levi smoothed out a wrinkle in the blanket and kept his gaze on the floor. The kid was a zombie, his head down and shoulders sagging. But what bothered Mr. Anderson the most, was the shame swimming in his eyes.

Mr. Anderson sighed. "I heard what happened. Some of it, anyway."

Levi glanced up, his mouth tight.

Mr. Anderson set a hand on the kid's shoulder, but the kid winced, so he removed it. "I'm really sorry about it, Levi."

Sorry wasn't enough, but again, Mr. Anderson was at a loss. All the kids he'd spoken to, all the speeches he'd given in classes, he'd never consoled a kid after defending himself from his own father. Again came the hot jab of anger, that a man could do this to his child. He wiped the back of his neck. "Levi, listen to me. None of this is your fault, you understand that, right?"

Levi nodded robotically, as though he didn't fully believe it but figured it best to go along for the instructor's sake. Regardless of whose fault it was, it had happened all the same. Then the kid's face changed, and he looked at him for the first time. "Mr. Anderson, I'm not sure how to say this, but I, tomorrow... I'm not, I don't think I can..." he trailed off.

From the moment he'd set foot in the house, Mr. Anderson had already decided that fighting was out. "Yeah, no, I get it. I completely understand, Levi. I wouldn't expect you to compete tomorrow. Not after this."

Levi nodded again, still staring at his feet. He exhaled, then went for the trash bag full of weapons, all packed and ready, laying on the floor beside the couch. He dragged it out and set it in front of his instructor.

"I really appreciate everything you've done for me. Honestly, I do. More than you know. I wish none of this had happened." He paused to wipe his eyes, his voice quivering. "I've enjoyed karate more than anything I've ever done, so, thanks."

Mr. Anderson was still staring at the trash bag when he caught the kid's meaning. "Wait, Levi. What is this?" Mr. Anderson said, flummoxed.

The kid nodded at the bag. "I just... I mean, with me not fighting at the tournament. I figured I wouldn't be able to come to karate anymore."

Levi's mother turned for the kitchen as though to hide her quiet sobbing. The boy, the trash bag, all of it hit Mr. Anderson right between the eyes, and he had to take a second to compose himself. "Levi, can we sit down?"

Levi was still staring at the bag as he nodded. "Yeah, sure."

They took a seat. Mr. Anderson remembered the day the kid had moved in, the happiness in the house and the coming and going of his mother's coworkers, how proud the kid had been of his new trophy. They'd moved there to hide, but they refused to lose hope, until it was stolen from them. If ever there was a time for his secret weapon, it was now. "You remember Margaret, right? Mrs. Keaton?"

Levi nodded, the faraway look in his eyes coming into focus.

Mr. Anderson continued. "You made quite an impression on her that day we came out."

Ms. Rocco appeared at the doorway again, clutching a tissue.

Mr. Anderson gave her a small smile. "You're not going anywhere, Levi. You hear me? Not even when you get your black belt."

Levi's eyes snapped open. He looked at his mother, then to Mr. Anderson. "But I thought, what Mr. Keaton said about..."

Mr. Anderson was already shaking his head. "You really think I'd let you quit? Nope. Overruled. Margaret Keaton owns Kick City. She made the call. She wants to start a scholarship program, and you are the first recipient."

The kid almost smiled. His eyes went glossy. "You mean, I can still come to class?"

"I mean that you *have* to come to class," Mr. Anderson said with a chuckle. With his foot, he slid the trash bag back toward Levi. Ms. Rocco was crying all over again. But this time they were quick hiccups of happiness. Mr. Anderson knew he couldn't fix what had happened, but he was happy to bring some kind of joy into this room.

The kid was up now, pacing, shaking his head and trying to make sense of it all. "She's going to, *you're* going to let me stay? Even if I can't fight tomorrow?"

"Yep, you've got many tournaments to win, Levi." He pointed to the fireplace. "That mantel is going to fill up fast."

Before he could finish the sentence, the kid dove into him with a hug.

CHAPTER THIRTY-NINE

Mr. Anderson smiled as Levi fixed his gi and adjusted his green belt. The kid was nervous, and to be honest, he was too. Today was big, bigger than anything he'd ever done before.

A few hundred people were in attendance for the grand ceremony of Maple Ridge Kick City's new location. The sun-faded *K* was perfect, as though it was meant to be all along. Mrs. Keaton had agreed. She'd okayed the project last spring.

The new space, 37,000 square feet sitting next door to the old space, gave them room for all sorts of activities. An indoor track. A demo room, sparring mats, even a yoga section— something Levi's mom planned to visit. And all the changes hadn't gone unnoticed. Membership was up fifty percent, not that Kenneth was there to see it.

Kenneth Keaton had resigned shortly after the Invitational tournament. The reason given for leaving the family business was to pursue a more lucrative career in accounting. It was for the best, Margaret had said, staring at the framed portrait of her husband as the demo team did their thing, she was ready to pursue more philanthropic efforts.

It was a banner day for Kick City as thirty-day passes flew around like confetti, the new studio was filled with ribbons and balloons and pageantry. Mr. Anderson's son was there, crawling around, drooling on the mats as Mr. Tabb guided a family tour through the new facility. Several times, Mr. Anderson had called Levi over and introduced him as their best sparrer before he had him demonstrate techniques. Other times the boy was called out by visitors who recognized him from the promos.

The kid had made strides even Mr. Anderson never dreamed of. He'd skipped a few belts and was well on track to be something special. He'd already won four tournaments and placed in several others.

And he'd visited his father.

Mr. Anderson had driven him to the prison when they happened to be nearby for a seminar. The kid hadn't seemed up for it at first, but in the weeks approaching, he'd warmed to the idea.

Mr. Anderson had remained in the lobby, of course, but Levi had said it went well. His father had apologized, for everything, and while it would be a long road to forgiveness and redemption, they had a few years before his father's release, so maybe there would be time to build some type of relationship between them.

But for now, the kid was all about karate. And Maple Ridge was booming.

As Levi won tournaments, and the girl kept the promotional videos rolling on the social channels, more and more kids showed up looking for the boy with the kicks. Turned out, Levi was not only a natural with his skills, but with teaching as well.

Levi got his belt tied. He smoothed out his gi when Mr. Anderson joked that one day, they might be rivals. The kid laughed, but then broke into a fighting stance.

Mr. Anderson raised an eyebrow. "Oh, so the student is ready to take on the teacher?"

The kid nodded, his smile beaming. Mr. Anderson took his position across the ring, knowing he'd rather be there than anyplace else in the world.

"Well, let's see what you got."

ACKNOWLEDGMENTS

Special thanks to Master Duval Davis III and Jaquell Watkins for the inspiration to write this story. Also, to the Super Kicks family in Forest, Virginia, where sitting through class after class this story was born. To Holli Anderson, Staci Olsen, Jason King and the entire Immortal Works family for taking on this story. To Diane Fanning, Wayne Fanning, Sue Fanning.

To Simon, for the kicks. To Bella for teaching me what really matters. And most of all, to Anne, for always believing.

Pete Fanning is the author of *Justice in a Bottle* and *Runaway Blues*. He lives in Virginia with his wife, son, baby girl, and two very spoiled dogs. He can be found at www.petefanning.com, where he's posted over 200 flash fiction stories.

This has been an
Immortal Production

9 781953 491848